"This must seem so boring to you, after all your travels."

"Hardly boring. And not all of them have been that exotic."

"Yeah, I'm sure. Just humdrum places like the Great Barrier Reef and Machu Pichu," she teased. Then she gestured at his sling. "Did you do that at a volcano or something?"

"Much closer to home, filming a piece on Yosemite National Park. I ended up smacking my collarbone on granite."

"Ouch."

Ouch indeed. It ached something fierce right now. Determined to ignore the throbbing, he took the box from her so he could carry it back to the barn.

"I'm glad you're okay…and that your life is exactly what you dreamed about. World travel, new adventures. I'm happy for you, Liam."

Much as he appreciated her words, her description of his dreams wasn't accurate. Before Dad died, Liam's visions of the future had included adventure, true, but the most important component of those dreams was having Clementine at his side.

Always and forever.

His swallow ached his throat. "Not everything goes according to plan, though."

Susanne Dietze began writing love stories in high school, casting her friends in the starring roles. Today, she's an award-winning, RWA RITA® Award–nominated author who's seen her work on the ECPA and *Publishers Weekly* bestseller lists for inspirational fiction. Married to a pastor and the mom of two, Susanne lives in California and enjoys fancy-schmancy tea parties, the beach and curling up on the couch with a costume drama. To learn more, say hi or sign up for her newsletter, visit her website, www.susannedietze.com.

Books by Susanne Dietze

Love Inspired

Widow's Peak Creek

A Future for His Twins
Seeking Sanctuary
A Small-Town Christmas Challenge
A Need to Protect

Love Inspired Historical

The Reluctant Guardian
A Mother for His Family

Visit the Author Profile page at LoveInspired.com.

A Need to Protect

Susanne Dietze

LOVE INSPIRED
INSPIRATIONAL ROMANCE

LOVE INSPIRED®

INSPIRATIONAL ROMANCE

Recycling programs
for this product may
not exist in your area.

ISBN-13: 978-1-335-75925-2

A Need to Protect

Copyright © 2022 by Susanne Dietze

For questions and comments about the quality of this book, please contact us
at CustomerService@Harlequin.com.

Love Inspired
22 Adelaide St. West, 41st Floor
Toronto, Ontario M5H 4E3, Canada
www.LoveInspired.com

Printed in U.S.A.

The Lord is my shepherd; I shall not want.
He maketh me to lie down in green pastures:
he leadeth me beside the still waters.
He restoreth my soul.
—*Psalm* 23:1–3

To Matthew, a true gift from God.
I'm so glad He made me your mom.

Acknowledgments

I am indebted to Lydia Tevis of Harmony Heritage
Farm for her tremendous help with my questions
about dairy sheep and her sheep milk soap.
Lydia's kindness and patience truly blessed me.
I'm also thankful to Jennifer Uhlarik
for lending her expertise when it came to
my drone questions and brainstorming
particular scenes with me. While these
two women were gracious to share with me,
I take full responsibility for any and all errors.

Thanks also to my editor, Emily Rodmell,
and the entire Love Inspired team;
to my agent, Tamela Hancock Murray;
and to my patient family, who cheer me on.

And to the Good Shepherd,
who keeps me in His flock.

Chapter One

"There's a man in the yard!"

At her four-year-old niece Annie's shout from the workshop door, Clementine Simon looked up from packaging bars of paper-wrapped lemongrass soap. It hadn't even been one minute since she'd left the kids alone so she could prepare the order—seven-year-old Wynn played with action figures in one of the fields, and Annie had been on the swing set right outside the workshop. Clementine wasn't expecting any visitors to the farm today, aside from an older woman from church who'd placed a soap order.

Definitely not a man.

Maybe the man in question was dropping off a delivery. Or he was a lost tourist, visiting Widow's Peak Creek for a weekend of exploring the Sierra Nevada foothills.

Or…he could be a creepy trespasser, slim though the possibility might be. Clementine's hometown was quiet, but as a single woman with two kids and twenty-odd sheep to protect, she didn't take chances.

"Let's go see who it is, then." Taking Annie's hand,

Clementine marched outside onto the driveway that dissected the fields from the house and other buildings.

Sure enough, a man in dark-rinse jeans, hiking-type boots and a charcoal-gray T-shirt, fitted just enough to reveal a muscular physique, rounded the hood of an unfamiliar black sedan. Once he was at the passenger side of the car, Clementine caught sight of his left arm, cradled against his chest in a black sling.

He assisted a tiny woman in a peony-pink tracksuit from the car, and Annie hopped at recognizing their expected guest, Marigold Murphy. "Hi, Mrs. Murphy!"

Clementine couldn't add her voice to Annie's, however, because her ability to speak, move or breathe vanished when the man turned his face toward her.

After all this time, he was back. Liam Murphy, Marigold's grandson.

The boy Clementine had never quite got over.

Not that he was a boy anymore, of course. It had been sixteen years since she closed the door on their relationship. Despite caring for one another, they'd been headed down different paths. He wanted a life of adventure, but she wanted to settle down and grow roots.

Parting ways was inevitable, so when his mom decided to move his family out of Widow's Peak Creek, Clementine agreed with her that it was best to make a clean break. Why invest in a long-distance relationship that wasn't going anywhere anyway?

Just because it was her choice, though, didn't mean it hadn't hurt. Telling Liam goodbye was one of the hardest things Clementine had ever experienced, second only to losing her sister two years ago, when she became guardian to Wynn and Annie.

Annie's hand slipped from Clementine's, dragging

her back to the present and renewing her ability to move. Nevertheless, walking several yards down the drive toward Liam, she felt like a newborn lamb taking its first steps on feeble legs.

Annie greeted Marigold with a hug. "Hi, Mrs. Murphy, did you bring mints?" It all came out in a rush, like one long word.

Marigold always shared the stash of butter mints from her purse with the kids during church, but Clementine would have to chat with Annie later about greeting guests.

"Hello, dear ones, and yes, I do have mints for you and Wynn." Marigold's excited voice was almost as high-pitched as Annie's. "Look who's here, Clementine. Are you surprised?"

"Very." Clementine congratulated herself for sounding almost normal, despite the shock his presence had done to her system. "Hi, Liam."

"Good to see you, Clementine." A lot about Liam had changed, from the way his hair swooshed over his brow to the trimmed beard he now sported. But not his smile, which made his dark eyes crinkle in a way she'd always found handsome. "You look great."

Yeah, right, with holes in her jeans and a chunk of blond hair loose from her scrunchie, blowing in the breeze against her nose. Self-consciously, she shoved the hair behind her ear. "So do you. Except for the sling, I mean. Sorry you're hurt. Broken arm?"

"Collarbone." His smiling gaze shifted to Annie. "Hi there."

Annie went uncharacteristically quiet. Clementine patted her head to reassure her. "Liam, this is Annie, my niece. Her brother Wynn is that running blur in blue."

Clementine gestured at the field to her left. "Annie, this is Mrs. Murphy's grandson, Liam Murphy."

Annie peered up at Clementine. "Has he been here before?"

"No, sweetheart."

"Welcome to Honeysuckle Farm," Annie said to him, parroting Clementine's usual greeting to first-time visitors and customers. "We grow sheep."

"I'll say." Liam's dark gaze flickered in amusement at Annie's word choice. He gestured at the grassy fields to his right. "The babies are cute."

"The babies are called lambs. They're boys and girls, but the big ones are all girls. Except for Scooter. He's a ram. And Dolley's a dog, but she's not a people-dog like Martha. Dolley keeps the co-dodies away."

"Yes, the *coyotes* don't want to tangle with Dolley." Clementine's correction was met with smiles.

Annie pointed out an ewe grazing near the fence line, surrounded by four lambs. "That's Frances."

Marigold chuckled. "Are all those lambs hers or did she borrow a few from a friend?"

"She had *quads*." Annie enunciated the word. "Dill, Sage, Basil and Nut."

"Nutmeg." Clementine met Marigold's smile.

"All boys, then? The girls are named for First Ladies," Marigold explained to Liam.

"Only the ones we keep." Clementine wished they could hold on to all the lambs, but it wasn't feasible. "Sage and Nutmeg are girls, but they're to be sold. The two females who are remaining with us did get First Lady names, though. Lucy and Abigail."

Annie's small hands fisted on her hips. "What about Bo Peep?"

"That's right, Bo Peep is the exception to our naming rule with lambs who stay."

"Because Wynn and I chose her for our own and we got to name her," Annie declared to her rapt audience. "We're gonna show her off at the festival."

"The county fair?" Liam's voice held a smile in it. "Fun."

"No, dear, this is something much smaller and brand-new this year." Marigold sounded as excited as Wynn and Annie about it. "It's called Gold Rush Days, celebrating Widow's Peak Creek and its history as an old gold rush town. It'll be at the fairgrounds, and Clementine's on the planning committee."

Not just on the committee. In charge of the vendor fair and the recipe contest and woefully behind on her to-do list. In fact, there wasn't a single entrant into the recipe contest yet, and the weekend-long festival was in five weeks. The stressful reminder sent Clementine's already rapid pulse accelerating.

She needed a second to breathe. "I was just packaging up your order when you pulled in, Marigold. I'll grab them from the soap shed. Be right back."

Walking to her workshop, she shoved her trembling hands into the front pockets of her jeans. *Liam's here, Lord*, she said silently to the Almighty, even though of course He knew. But she talked to God about everything, and He didn't seem to mind if she stated the obvious.

Why had Liam come back? He hadn't visited Marigold in years. None of her business, but boy, seeing him again sure affected her. Even after all this time. Good thing she'd have a minute to compose herself while she grabbed the soaps.

"Clemmie!"

At the shout, she turned around. Wynn rushed over the grass toward her, and his lack of smile told her he wasn't running because he saw Marigold and was excited for butter mints. Something wasn't right.

She jogged back across the driveway to meet him. "Wynn?"

He stopped at the woven-wire railing where Marigold and Liam stood. "Hi, Mrs. Murphy. Sir." He turned a worried gaze to Clementine. "It's Mr. Campbell. One of the ewes got through a tear in the fence. He pointed at Eleanor."

Clementine's stomach sank to the soles of her canary sneakers. There was a lot to handle in those few sentences of Wynn's. First things first, though.

"Are you all right, Wynn?" Fergus Campbell, their new neighbor to the east, was not the friendliest fellow. He'd barked at Annie last week when she leaned on the perimeter fence to watch him work.

"I'm fine." Already Wynn sounded less winded.

"Eleanor must have been curious," Annie said. *Curious* was an often-used word, now that she'd started enjoying books about the inquisitive monkey and the man with the yellow hat.

Clementine's six East Friesian ewes and lone ram didn't tend to be intrigued by anything beyond the grain bucket, however. And the perimeter fence had seemed fine when Clementine checked it a week ago. What could have caused a tear large enough for a sheep to get through?

Regardless, Clementine had to repair the breach fast before more members of her little flock ventured onto Fergus Campbell's property.

"I'm sorry, but I'd better talk to my neighbor and repair the fence. Mr. Campbell is new to town, and I'm already on his bad side." Clementine's gaze met Liam's for the briefest of moments before skittering to Marigold. "I'll grab your soap first, so you can be on your way."

"The soap can wait. How can I help, Clem?" Liam's old nickname for her took her right back to high school.

He was kind to offer, but surely he was only being polite. "Thanks, but you two have much better things to do."

"We haven't planned a thing. Don't let his broken collarbone fool you, Clementine. His one arm is plenty strong." Marigold took Annie's hand. "What pretty nail polish, dear."

"It's pink." Like everything else on Annie, from her T-shirt to her tennis shoes. "It's the kind that peels off. Clemmie says I have to be in kindergarten before I get the stay-on kind."

"Maybe you can paint my nails with your special polish while Clemmie and Liam fix the fence. And Wynn, you can tell me all about school." Marigold shooed her hand at Clementine and Liam, like they were mosquitoes. "You two go on. We're fine here."

Clementine's protests died on her lips as Marigold and the kids hurried into the house. Was Marigold trying to be helpful by watching the kids, or was this what it felt like to be railroaded into spending time alone with Liam? Marigold was, after all, one of Widow's Peak Creek's most notorious—and effective—matchmakers.

She shouldn't have bothered. Clementine had broken up with Liam when she was eighteen because they were headed in different directions. Nothing had changed. For him, work kept him on the road most of the year, and "business trips" meant venturing to the depths of underground caves, the heights of Mount Everest and dangers at every elevation in between as a camera operator for nature documentaries.

He led a fascinating life, sure, but when—if—she was ever in a place to be in a relationship again, it would be with someone who didn't rappel down cliffs or get up close and personal with wild animals as part of his job.

Someone who wasn't a risk-taking adrenaline junkie who could one day get in an accident and leave her alone, the way her sister had.

Grandma was about as subtle as the elephant bull that had charged Liam's film crew in Botswana last year. There was no mistaking her intentions or how hard she'd tried to conceal them until they'd driven into Clementine's driveway. All he'd been told was she had errands.

Liam didn't appreciate Grandma's brazen intervention, but all the same, he couldn't help but feel grateful for the opportunity to talk to Clementine after sixteen years, just converse like two people who used to know one another and could still be cordial. That way, when she came to mind in the future, he'd have a memory of her that didn't throb like an old wound when the weather changed.

Following a quick stop in the raised-center-aisle-style barn to grab her tool kit and a roll of green plastic, they strode across a field dotted with groups of wooly white sheep. Every so often, a lamb kicked its legs and leaped, and it was impossible not to smile at the display of unbridled joy. Maybe talking about the sheep would be a good way to break the ice. "First Lady names, huh?"

"Frances, Eleanor, Julia, Lady Bird, Mary and Mamie. Fifteen lambs among them this year."

"How old are they? The lambs, I mean."

"Between three and five weeks old. Of the fifteen, we're still bottle feeding nine."

He hadn't missed her use of the word *we*, and he was pretty sure she wasn't strictly referring to herself and the kids. It must be a holdover from the days when she lived here with Brielle and Brad, her sister and brother-in-law.

Grandma had filled him in on the tragic circumstances surrounding their deaths two years ago. Who would ever have expected an avalanche on the slope they were skiing? Talk about a freak accident. Since Clementine's parents did church work in Uganda, she'd been chosen as the kids' legal guardian.

A large, fluffy dog, the same hue as the sheep, trotted over, black nose twitching in Liam's direction. As a dog lover, Liam itched to greet her, but if this was the flock guardian Annie had mentioned, it might be in his best interest to get acquainted on the dog's terms. "Annie said her name's Dolley, right? How do I let her know I'm not a threat to the sheep?"

"She knows already. Her main concern is coyotes, but with people and domesticated animals, she's a sweetheart. So good with the kids, too, but she views the flock as her tribe."

Liam allowed Dolley to investigate his hand. Then he stroked the soft, thick fur behind her floppy ears. Dolley's mouth opened in a way that looked like a smile. A high-pitched *meh* from one of the lambs got Dolley's attention, and she sauntered off toward it. Liam couldn't help but grin. "She's one big dog."

"A true gentle giant. The sheep feel secure to munch grass and snooze and produce good milk for me."

"That's right. You make soap with the milk. I'd never heard of that before." Goat-milk soap, yes, but not sheep.

"I sell extra milk to a local cheesemaker and make a few items with the wool, but soap is my mainstay. Your grandma is one of my best customers. Now I know why she wanted to come by today when I could've handed her order to her at church tomorrow. She must be so excited you're here for the weekend." She glanced at him through the curtain of blond hair that had slipped from her ponytail.

He tried not to stare. How could he have forgotten how blue her eyes were, deep and pure as the sky just after dawn? Or how pretty she looked in spring colors like her peachy V-neck T-shirt. Not to say she hadn't changed since high school. She was just as beautiful, but the faintest of lines rimmed those eyes now. She wore confidence like a shawl about her shoulders, and her chin tipped up as though she was ready to face whatever came next.

Which reminded him, she'd said *weekend.* "About my visit, Clem—"

"Two times in less than two weeks, missy." A man stomped toward them from the opposite side of the shoulder-high perimeter fence. Lanky, white-bearded and clad head to toe in denim, he bent forward as if he were being pushed from behind by a stiff wind.

"Sorry, Fergus." Clementine's head tipped to the side. "Wynn said Eleanor snuck through. Did she do any damage to your property?"

"I scared her off first." Fergus adjusted his large bifocals. "It's a big hole in the fence she got through, missy."

"I apologize for not catching it. Rex clearly missed it on his rounds, too."

Who was Rex? Liam didn't like the way his brain rushed to that question when there were a thousand other things of greater import going on right now.

Like the way Fergus narrowed his eyes at Clementine. "Seems like you two are letting things slip, if you ask me."

Wait, what was this guy suggesting? Clementine was negligent? This was none of Liam's business, but the Clementine he'd always known was scrupulous. The fence, made of woven wire and wood posts, was weathered but sturdy-looking to Liam. Fergus was out of line. "That's taking a hole in a fence too far, don't you think?"

"Who are you?" Fergus squinted at Liam.

"Thanks for your concern, Fergus." Clementine didn't give Liam an opportunity to answer Fergus's question. "I take my obligations seriously, so I'd better make that repair now. Have a good day."

"Be glad that big dog of yours didn't come onto my property. If it attacked my chickens, there'd be trouble."

"She doesn't attack chickens."

Fergus turned around, muttering as he hobbled, like his knees caused him pain, toward a ranch-style farmhouse in need of a paint job.

"Wait." Frustration filled Liam's chest. "Where's the hole?"

When Fergus didn't acknowledge them, Clementine shrugged. "It has to be in this field because the sheep have been in here all day. Since Wynn didn't notice Eleanor go or come while he was playing out here, it's probably behind those cottonwoods." She tipped her head to their left, farther north along the fence line.

Made sense. They walked beneath the cluster of trees, and sure enough, a segment of fence had detached from a wood post, leaving a flap large enough for a sheep to pass through. Or a predator. "How does something like this happen?"

Clementine examined the post and edge of the fence. "The staples are gone."

"Like someone pulled them out? You said Dolley isn't interested in people, right? So, she wouldn't have paid attention to a human intruder?"

"Her training extends to anything out of the ordinary, and she definitely would've barked at a nocturnal visit like that. Who would make a tear in a random section of my fence, though? There's no good reason for opening a hole here unless someone wanted to crawl between my house and Fergus's. No, that's ridiculous." She rubbed her forehead, like the puzzle of the fence made it ache. "We had wind a few nights ago. It must've been stronger than I thought. The fence was old when Brielle and Brad bought the place."

It still seemed odd to Liam, but admittedly, he was no fence expert. "How can I help?"

"Dig out my pliers, if you don't mind." Gloves on, she tugged the gaping fence farther away from the wood post.

The pliers were easy to find, and when he handed them over, she clipped the vertical end wire all the way down. Then she tugged what looked like a knot made of wire from the top of the fence. "Hold out your hand." She dropped the knot in his palm. "There's going to be a few more. Stick them in your pocket."

"So you can use them again?"

"So no one steps on them or eats them."

This was a good example of why he hadn't settled down and become a parent. The idea that a small human or animal would stick a sharp object in his or her mouth? Totally foreign to him. Good thing he realized a long time ago that he wasn't meant to have a family.

As he pocketed the sharp pieces of wire, she unfurled the roll of green plastic. "I'm going to overlap the pieces. Hold this end in place while I secure it to the original fencing here and on the other side of the post."

"Got it." He held his end taut while she made quick work of securing it to the wire fence with zip ties. "Who's Rex?"

He could've kicked himself for blurting out the question.

"He lends a hand twice a week. Honorary grandpa to the kids."

Liam shouldn't feel relieved at her answer, but he did. "Sounds like a good arrangement."

"It is. I'll ask him to check fencing on Monday when he's here." With a snap, she secured the final zip tie. "I'm saving up for electric fencing, but this will hold for now."

He returned the pliers to the toolbox. "You're adept at this."

"I've had some practice." She jiggled her handiwork, flashing him a small smile. "This must seem so boring to you after all your travels through exotic locales."

"Hardly boring. And not all of them have been that exotic."

"Yeah, I'm sure. Just humdrum places like the Great Barrier Reef and Machu Picchu," she teased. Then she gestured at his sling. "Did you do that at a volcano or something?"

"Much closer to home, filming a piece on Yosemite National Park, while climbing up Half Dome. I slipped, tried to protect the camera and ended up smacking my collarbone on granite."

"Ouch." She shut the toolbox with a metallic clink.

Ouch, indeed. It ached something fierce right now, reminding him he was due for some over-the-counter pain medication. Determined to ignore the throbbing, he took the box from her so he could carry it back to the barn. "Thankfully, I was cabled in, or it could've been a lot worse."

"I'm glad you're okay…and that your life is exactly what you dreamed about. World travel, new adventures. I'm happy for you, Liam."

Much as he appreciated her words, her description of his dreams wasn't accurate. Before Dad died and Mom announced they were leaving Widow's Peak Creek, Liam's visions of the future did include adventure, true, but the most important component of those dreams was Clementine at his side.

Always and forever.

His swallow ached his throat. "Not everything goes according to plan, though."

"I'm proof of that. This was not the life I pictured." She gestured at the sheep.

"This might not have been your plan, Clementine, but I'm not the least bit surprised you're caring for Brielle's kids or running a successful business that incorporates your lifelong love of animals and agriculture. Honeysuckle Farm is beautiful, truly."

He didn't exaggerate. The acreage, divided into a half

dozen fenced enclosures, was blanketed in lush, sweet-smelling grass, except for the gravel path between the fields and the barn. He didn't know much about barns, but he liked the style, with its two-story high center and one-story lean-tos on either side, flanked by an open-air shelter, all painted traditional red. The white house was a good architectural complement, with its black shutters and red brick accents.

A refreshing spring breeze ruffled through the leaves of the elms and ash trees in the fields as well as the cottonwoods planted around the property's perimeter. New leaves budded on fruit trees between the two-story house and the barn, not far from the swing set and furnished outdoor patio, which Clementine had decorated with pots of spring blooms. Back toward the street, a fenced area between the road and the sheep looked like it was full of berry bushes and a vegetable garden.

This was a well-loved home, and though Liam was not one to settle down, the place was inviting.

Clementine's gaze scanned the fence line. "I can't take any credit for the property. Brad and Brielle did all the hard work fixing it up when they bought it. Some things were not in good shape, but they couldn't resist buying it, because of the creek."

"Widow's Peak Creek runs through here?" He'd always believed the waterway that gave the town its name flowed east of here and never on personal property. Neighborhoods were built around the creek, abutting it. Not through it.

"No, it's a small tributary, Blue Creek." She shoved the tendril of hair behind her ear again. "It forks off the big creek on the city-owned nature preserve across that fence, runs through the northern end of my property and ends in a ponding basin beneath those trees."

"What a bonus." He'd noticed the trees growing thicker in the northwest corner of her land, in line with the house and a few small outbuildings. If he were the sort of person who'd been made to grow roots, he might have wanted a place like this, where he could dip his toes in the creek on hot summer days and enjoy the view of the Sierra Nevada.

But he was too restless to stay in one place. Too unsatisfied. Too broken. Better to stay busy, without the spare time to deal with any emotional issues.

Unfortunately, he had nothing but time on his hands during his upcoming stay in Widow's Peak Creek. Time and reminders of the past.

Which jogged his memory... He hadn't finished filling Clementine in on his visit. "I know my coming to your farm was a surprise to both of us, but I'm glad we could reconnect like this. Just us, talking, rather than awkwardly running into each other on Main Street or something."

"I agree. If she hadn't brought you, I might not have known you were in town until after you'd left. I mean, you're here for the weekend, right? Leaving tomorrow?"

"Not quite. I had surgery a few days ago. I can't operate my equipment until I've fully recovered. It'll take six weeks, according to the doctor, so I'm staying in the tiny house Grandma and her neighbor rent out."

"Six weeks? You won't be here the whole time, though. I mean, you've got a home base in Los Angeles, right?"

"The casita at Sara's house." His older sister. "But she and Dane, that's her husband— Well, it's not important. It's been too long since I've spent time with Grandma, so here I am."

It was impossible to tell from her blank expression how she felt about the prospect of seeing him around town for over a month. At least she didn't seem angry, just stunned. Then, blinking, she brushed past him into the barn. "If you just had surgery, you shouldn't have been helping me."

"All I did was hand you pliers and hold plastic in place." He set the toolbox down on the workbench and then dug into his pocket for the metal pieces she'd given him.

"Does it hurt? Your collarbone?"

"Yeah." He would've shrugged if it didn't ache so much. "But I've hurt worse."

Her sharp gaze met his, questioning. Almost wounded. Like she thought he'd referred to the pain she'd caused him at their breakup.

He hadn't been, but if he were being honest?

Yeah, he'd take the stabbing pain of a broken collarbone over how she'd dumped him any day.

Chapter Two

Clementine turned away on the pretext of throwing the sharp wire clippings into the trash, but she was glad to have a reason to look away from Liam.

When she broke up with him all those years ago, she was heartbroken, but she'd trusted God had a plan for her. It turned out His plan took her in a direction she never would have envisioned—namely that she'd be thirty-four, unmarried, raising Brielle's kids—but He'd been faithful through it all. She needed to focus on what He was doing in and through her, not what might have been.

Did Liam struggle from their breakup? Or find it impossible to forgive her? Probably not. She mustn't assume his comment about the suffering he'd experienced had to do with her ending their relationship years ago. After all, Liam was such an adrenaline junkie, he'd probably broken a dozen bones. Surely one of them had caused greater pain than their teenage breakup.

Perspective set, she turned back. "I hope helping with the fence didn't aggravate your injury."

"Nah, but I'm ready to ice it when I get back to Grandma's."

"Speaking of Marigold, I think we'd better check on her before Annie decides to paint her toenails, too." She led him out of the barn. "I'll pop into the soap shed for her order and then you guys can be on your way."

"Thanks, Clementine."

She could tell he wasn't just talking about the soap. The fact that they could have a normal-ish conversation wasn't a small thing. This opportunity to talk showed her he was happy. Healthy, except for that collarbone. He'd moved on and led a life that fulfilled him.

Maybe now, in the deepest recesses of her heart, she could finally let him go. Or at a minimum, make a real start at it.

"Thank you, too, Liam."

It might be weird having him around town for over a month, but at least they'd first met up in private. Not that she felt completely at peace, of course. Being around him made her insides buzz like she'd swallowed a beehive.

But honestly, it was doubtful she'd see much of him, if she saw him at all. Their paths were unlikely to cross again, even in a town the size of Widow's Peak Creek.

She slept poorly that night due to an unexpected rain shower passing through, but naturally, her brain decided that the wee hours were the perfect time to process her encounter with Liam. After a few hours of tossing and turning, she drifted off again just in time to be jolted awake by the peppy electronic tune of her 5:00 a.m. alarm. Of course.

She was groggy and unfocused during her Sunday

morning chores, feeding both sheep and children, so it wasn't until an icy plink hit her atop the head while she was milking the eldest ewe, Lady Bird, that she realized the barn roof was leaking.

How could she have missed the puddle in the milking stanchion? Rubbing her eyes and whispering a prayer for patience, she mopped, set a bucket beneath the drips and returned to the house to get dressed for church. They were behind schedule, so if she had to put her lipstick and blush on in the car while she was stopped at red lights, so be it. She shoved her feet into her low heels and grabbed her purse. "Come on, guys. We're going to be late."

"My shoes don't fit," Wynn complained.

By the time they handled the shoe problem, got to church, signed the kids into the children's activity and she slipped into the sanctuary of Good Shepherd Church, the opening hymn was in its final verse.

Clementine scoured the seats. Great. The only place left to sit was in the front pew. As she made her way up the side aisle, she passed her usual spot, where Marigold and Liam had found seats. It was hard not to feel self-conscious, knowing Liam was here in church and able to see her. She'd worn her hair up, and she resisted the urge to touch the back of her neck to check if the tag of her yellow floral dress stuck out. Or if—

Stop. She was in church. God more than deserved her attention and praise, so she shut her eyes and focused on Pastor Benton's sermon.

She managed to concentrate on God until the kids rejoined her after the children's activity. After showing her the projects they'd made, both Annie and Wynn turned around to wave enthusiastically at Marigold. They were probably hoping for butter mints.

"You can chat later, guys," she whispered, guiding them to face forward. Liam met her gaze with an amused, sweet smile that in another time would have given her heart palpitations.

Okay, maybe it still did, because her heart rate was skyrocketing. Much as she hated to admit it, she'd been hyperaware of Liam Murphy since she was fifteen years old. Even before they'd dated, she'd noticed his clothes and the way his dark hair waved in the back. Some habits were hard to break, but it was time to stop that nonsense.

After the service, Marigold and Liam were immediately approached by some of Marigold's friends, so Clementine and the kids exited the sanctuary without interrupting them. The children went straight for the snack table set up beneath the oak tree on the patio, and Clementine kept a careful eye on them while she exchanged greetings with friends. The kids seemed content to munch on cookies in the company of their peers until the Murphys arrived on the sunny patio. They ran to Marigold, weaving through the crowd.

Clementine excused herself from the group of moms she'd been conversing with and made her way across the patio.

"They pinched my toes," Wynn was explaining to Marigold, sticking out his right foot. "Clemmie said my feet must've grown this week because my shoes were fine last Sunday. My other shoes were too dirty for church so Clemmie let me wear sandals today."

"Good thing the weather's warm enough." Marigold dug into her purse, then withdrew a worn baggie chock-full of butter mints. "I far prefer my toes to be free than pinched in fancy shoes."

Liam's smile slanted in a teasing look. "Maybe you need different shoes, Grandma. I'll get you a good pair of hiking boots if you want. I wear them all the time." Then he flashed his grin Clementine's way. "Good morning."

"Hi." Hiking boots might be his daily choice, but today, he'd dressed for church in a crisp white dress shirt, chinos and leather loafers. She tried not to dwell on the subtle, delicious scent swirling around him, which was familiar yet intriguing when blended with the products he must use. Was it cologne or—

Clementine shut down that line of thinking. She smoothed her nephew's dark blond cowlick, which got his attention. "You know what growing feet mean, and Easter's almost here."

Wynn's shoulders sank. "Shoe shopping."

"I want to go shoe shopping," Annie said.

"A girl after my own heart." Marigold's laugh was high and sweet.

Annie selected a pastel yellow butter mint from Marigold's bag. "I like shoeboxes, too. They're good for keeping treasures in, like my rocks. I have a bunch of red ones from the creek."

While Annie regaled Marigold with a story about her collection of reddish rocks, Liam turned toward Clementine, his sleeve brushing against hers. "I tried your soap. It's nice."

Aha, that was what she smelled. "Patchouli Cedarwood?"

"You can smell it? Did I use too much?" A look of horror replaced his easy smile.

"No, I'm just, um, accustomed to the aroma of the essential oils I use for the soaps." Except it smelled way different on his skin than it did as a bar. *Talk about something else, fast.* "It's nice of you to come to church today."

"Why wouldn't I?"

"Why would you?" He wasn't a churchgoing guy. "Other than to spend time with Marigold."

He looked down at the stained concrete beneath them, a small smile playing about his lips. "About a year ago, I was on a crew filming in Mexico, inside an underground cavern. The only access was through a narrow, vertical shaft. Fifty feet down. There was a problem with my gear, and I swung wide on the cable and hit my head against the shaft wall."

"Oh, Liam." This job of his sounded even more dangerous than she'd imagined. She'd never watch a documentary the same way again. "That's terrible."

"When I came to, I was still dangling halfway down. While my team members scrambled to get me back up, I realized I couldn't save myself. Not literally, in that moment, or spiritually. I came to faith thanks to a bonk on the head."

Clementine couldn't erase from her mind the horrifying image of him hitting his head. "I'm so glad to hear that, Liam, but you could've died."

"I didn't, though."

But he could've. Had it really been worth the risk? Brielle and Brad disregarded safety to take a risk two years ago, by skiing in a closed area, and they'd paid for their choice with their lives.

His brow furrowed. "You're cross with me."

She took a deep breath. "No. Just…that's quite a

story." And she was focusing on the wrong part of it. "I'm glad you came to know God. Really."

"I'm still learning. Still struggling with some things, some things I find it hard to forgive, but that's the journey, I guess."

Forgive? Yesterday, she'd read too much into things Liam said, but she couldn't help but wonder if she was one of those things he struggled with forgiving.

"Liam Murphy, is that you behind that beard?" A redheaded woman in a kelly green shirtdress wedged herself between Clementine and Liam.

"Gretchen Weinbach." Liam's eyes lit up at seeing his old chemistry partner from high school.

They were both a year younger than Clementine, which meant she hadn't shared classes with them, but she'd always suspected Gretchen had a huge crush on Liam. Clementine didn't blame her. She'd had one herself.

"We hear you're a fancy filmmaker." Gretchen waved her hands jazz-style. "Is there a story behind that broken arm?"

"Collarbone, and I don't know about fancy," Liam said. "I love my job, though."

"I want the scoop, but I'm late to brunch. I couldn't leave without saying hey, though."

Clementine wasn't part of the conversation, and the kids were undoubtedly hungry for lunch. She took a half step back, ready to tell Marigold goodbye, when Gretchen turned on the balls of her nude heels and pinned her with a glare.

"You haven't emailed me any updates yet."

"I planned to fill in the committee at tomorrow's meeting." She glanced at a confused-looking Liam.

"Gretchen's the head of the Gold Rush Days team. She keeps the rest of us volunteers in line."

Gretchen didn't appear the least bit appeased by Clementine's praise. "I don't like being blindsided, Clementine."

"I didn't mean to give you the impression I was holding anything back. There just hasn't been much to tell. Last night, I received our first entrants to the cooking contest, and I started work on a chart for vendor placement—"

"Started to? The festival's in five weeks. Sounds to me like you need help."

Much as she hated to admit it, Clementine could use assistance with her festival tasks. Her responsibilities with the cooking contest and vendor fair would only increase the closer they got to the festival. She had plenty to do at home, too, with the kids and sheep, and it also appeared her perimeter fence wasn't as secure as she'd thought. Then there was the matter of her barn roof leaking.

Clementine rubbed her forehead. "You're right. I'll ask around."

It was impossible to miss the way Marigold nudged Liam's midsection with her elbow.

His lips twitched. "Are you volunteering me, Grandma?"

"Not necessarily." Marigold's shrug and wide eyes conveyed innocent intentions. "But you're so active, you might appreciate having something to do. You told Benton you'd go to the men's Bible study on Wednesdays, but that's the only thing on your docket that I know of."

"Say yes." Gretchen's voice returned to the honeyed tone she used for Liam. "We've got a meeting tomorrow morning. Ten a.m. sharp at Clementine's house. Can you make it?"

Liam's inscrutable gaze met Clementine's, as if awaiting her word on the subject.

She couldn't say her first thoughts, though. Marigold was a known matchmaker, and if her objective was to push them together? Her efforts were not welcome and would prove fruitless.

But how could she say no to the offer of help? This was about the festival, after all. Not her.

Except Liam helping with Gold Rush Days would affect her. Despite the peace she'd felt at their parting yesterday, her pounding heart and self-consciousness around him told her there was still more work to be done when it came to getting over the past. Over him or the memory of him that still pained her heart.

Maybe, Lord, more time in his company will be an opportunity for complete healing.

And maybe he needed closure, too. Probably not, since he was happy, living his dream. But he mentioned that he struggled with some things, like forgiveness. She couldn't help but feel this was something she should agree to.

Her nod was small, but it was enough for Liam to understand she was okay with his help. He looked back at Gretchen. "I don't know anything about festivals, but I can make flyers or phone calls. Anything that doesn't take two arms." He glanced at his sling. "Count me in as Clementine's assistant."

"Aren't you the best?" Gretchen grinned and patted his elbow. "Don't you think so, Clementine?"

She nodded. "It'll be a big help."

And it would, even if being around him caused

some awkwardness. If it allowed for complete closure, though, partnering with him on a few festival tasks was a small price to pay.

Then, in a few weeks when the festival was over, she could close the door on her long-ago love for Liam Murphy, once and for all.

An hour after leaving church, Liam returned the ice pack he'd been holding to his collarbone to the freezer. Better.

The clattering of utensils drew him back around. "Here, let me do that, Grandma." He took the cutlery from her hand, kissing her cheek as he did so. "I can set the table."

"Thanks, sweetheart." Grandma carried a large bowl of her Italian-style pasta salad to the table, placing it beside a basket of fragrant yeast rolls.

Once they'd thanked God for His blessings, Liam eagerly took a roll and slathered it with butter. "No one makes rolls like you do, Grandma."

"You're good for my ego, Liam."

"Good thing I'm living next door for a while, then?" he teased.

"I'll say, even if you do have a beard." Grandma shut her eyes in a mock look of despair. "You have the sweetest dimples, but now they're hidden under all those whiskers."

"It's easier not to have to shave every day when I'm on the road. And hey, Grandpa had a mustache, so either you secretly hated it or you're just giving me a hard time."

"I'll leave that a mystery." Smiling to herself, she spooned herself a portion of pasta salad. "How's the tiny house? Will it work for you?"

"It's great. You guys did an amazing job with it."
Grandma and her next-door neighbors Kellan and Paige
Lambert co-owned the compact, two-story dwelling
that straddled their property lines. The tiny house was
perfect to host visiting family, but they also received
income on it, renting it out to tourists. He would have
been happy staying with Grandma in her house, but
she'd insisted he'd appreciate privacy during his six-
week stay in Widow's Peak Creek.

It might be small, but it was comfortable and quiet.
Grandma had decorated the interior in neutrals with
pops of bright color, and the outside matched the charm-
ing arts-and-crafts architectural style of the neighborhood. He had no complaints, but in truth, he hadn't yet
unpacked his luggage. He was so accustomed to living
out of suitcases that it felt weird to place his socks in
an actual drawer.

He didn't plan to spend much time in the tiny house
anyway. "Do you have any projects for me while I'm
here?"

"You just had surgery, dear one. The doctor said light
activities, remember?"

Grandma's remark was almost laugh-out-loud funny,
considering how she'd volunteered him to help fix a
fence and do who-knew-what for a festival. "I think
I can manage yard work, Grandma." He dug into the
pasta salad. Delicious, with cubes of mozzarella cheese,
chunks of chicken, fresh vegetables, and parsley and
basil from her garden.

"We'll see. You might be busier once you connect
with people at the men's Bible study breakfasts. You
and Benton were kids together, but others are new to
town, like Joel Morgan—he's a lawyer who helped

Clementine with the legal issues when she got guardianship of the kids. Didn't charge her a dime. And you'll like getting to know Kellan better. He's on the festival committee, too."

"They both sound like good guys." But she'd changed the subject. "I mean it, Grandma. Let me help around here."

"I can't think of anything I need a hand with, but one of these days, I'd love to see that drone camera thingamabob you brought. So would Clementine and the kids, I bet." Her tone was pointedly casual.

He wasn't fooled. "You don't have an ulterior motive when it comes to me and Clementine, do you?"

"All I did was suggest two children might enjoy watching your robot camera flying around." She whirled her hand in a circle like a helicopter's blades.

Robot camera. He'd have to share that with the rest of the crew. "That's fine, but don't get your sights set on anything else between me and Clementine."

"Like what?" She glanced up from her pasta, as if she didn't know what he was talking about.

"Like rekindling our teenage romance. Clementine and I are old news. So is the fact that I'm not getting married. Ever. And you know the reason why."

Chapter Three

Liam hated that he'd caused the resigned look that creased Grandma's gentle face, but he'd had to make himself clear. "I'm sorry to put it like that, but I'm single for a reason."

"Because of your parents." Grandma pushed a cube of mozzarella around her plate with her fork. "It breaks my heart that you've allowed their marriage to cast such a long shadow."

Allowed it? From his perspective, his parents' behavior had completely molded his impressions of matrimony. Dad had hidden away in his sculpting studio, leaving Mom to stew in her anger. Mom had always complained they didn't fit into each other's worlds and never should've tried. They hadn't spent time together, other than to argue.

Granted, his long-suffering dad had offered to get counseling. To work things out.

Mom had been another story, though, threatening divorce on a weekly basis. Until Dad was diagnosed with a rare blood cancer, that is. After that, Liam saw love in his parents' eyes, and a lot of regret, too.

Through it all, Liam and Sara had been optimistic about relationships. Their futures wouldn't echo their parents' unhappy marriage. Love could conquer all, and in fact, after his dad's diagnosis, their parents had started to grow together again.

But Dad's passing was swift, and right after the funeral, Mom had announced they were leaving town. She wanted a clean slate, even though it meant uprooting Liam right before his senior year in high school. His only consolation had been that he wouldn't lose Clementine. A year older than he was, she was heading off for college, so he knew they'd be separated. Their relationship would endure, though. His love for Clementine was real. Strong.

But he'd been an idiot for being so certain, so optimistic that things would be different for him, because Clementine had dumped him the night before he left Widow's Peak Creek. Love, it turned out, was too much trouble for her. Not worth fighting for at all.

His older sister Sara, however, had retained her hopefulness. She fell in love and thought she'd make a go of it. Lately, though, her marriage had grown complicated. Her husband, Dane, wanted kids. Kids Sara wasn't sure she was equipped to raise.

What if I have kids and am that sort of parent? Sara never asked it aloud, but Liam recognized the look in his sister's eyes when the topic came up, because he had the same fear. What if he was angry, like his mom, or distant, like his dad? It wasn't worth finding out. Not when children's lives could be damaged.

Grandma couldn't understand, though. She may have seen his parents' marriage fracture, but she hadn't lived in the house with them, unable to escape the arguments and tension. And in her own life, she'd loved one man,

Grandpa. They'd had a beautiful life. Her heart had never been broken, until his death.

How to explain it to her?

"I know not every marriage is as bad as my parents' was, Grandma, and that's good for those people. But not me. I don't know how to be any different."

"By being yourself, silly." Grandma's white eyebrows pulled low into a vexed line. "Your dad—well, I loved my son dearly, but he'd get so consumed with his sculptures that he wasn't as attentive as he should've been. I understand why your mom grew bitter, even though I was devastated when she left with you and Sara. In any case, you are your own person."

True, but that didn't mean marriage was for him. Grandma meant well, though, and he loved her all the more for it. "I'm happy to help Clementine, but don't expect romance, okay? With her or anyone."

She sniffed. "If it's a decision you made with the Lord, who am I to interfere?"

He'd never thought of it that way. Maybe God had a different life plan charted for Liam. He doubted it, though. He had an excellent job he enjoyed that was a perfect fit to his adventurous nature and bachelor state.

His stay in Widow's Peak Creek would be brief, and then he could go back to living out of a suitcase again. Without a woman or kids who needed him.

Life was a lot easier, and less painful, that way.

After a dinner out that evening, Liam and his grandma strolled beside the creek that gave the town its name, flowing as it did into a telltale V shape around a huge boulder in Hughes Park. Seeing the familiar landmark felt like greeting an old friend. Something inside him relaxed, like he'd come home.

Ridiculous. It had been half a lifetime since he'd lived here. *What I'm feeling is nothing but nostalgia, right, Lord? Help me keep proper perspective so I'm mentally prepared for where You take me next.*

He continued a variation of the prayer the next morning when he knocked on Clementine's black-painted front door. *Proper perspective.* He'd thought he'd forgiven Clementine for ending things the way she had, but he lacked peace. Peace would be a good thing to have before he left town again, and he braced himself for Clementine to open the door.

To his surprise, a solidly built older fellow welcomed him into a white entrance hall furnished with a navy blue–painted bench and credenza. The man's gray eyes curved into smiling crescents, and deep wrinkles etched his cheeks and brow from years of working outdoors. "Come on in. Here for the Gold Rush Days thingamabob?"

Funny—Grandma had said *thingamabob* yesterday. Liam hadn't heard the word in years, and now, twice in twenty-four hours? It must be a Widow's Peak Creek thing he'd never noticed before. "Sure am. I'm Liam Murphy."

"Ah, Marigold's boy. I'm Rex Rigsby. I help Clementine with odds and ends." The older man thrust out his work-rough hand for a shake.

"You know my grandma?"

"Oh, she's the finest gal in the county."

She was indeed, but was that a blush creeping up from beneath Rex's brown plaid collar?

Mumbling something about a dentist appointment, Rex exited in a red-faced hurry. Was there something going on between this guy and Grandma? He'd have to ask her later. But for now, chatting voices and the rich aroma of fresh-brewed coffee drew him deeper into the house. Ahead, in a black-and-white great room, half a dozen people gathered on cozy-looking furniture. He caught Clementine's gaze at the same moment a thigh-high bundle of golden fur barreled into his legs, all tail-waggling canine energy.

This dog wasn't pale blond Dolley that kept company with the sheep. This one was a golden retriever, her white muzzle attesting to her advancing age. Liam dropped to bended knee to greet her. "You're a pretty girl, aren't you?"

Clementine snickered as the dog flopped into a belly-up puddle at his feet. "Martha should have gone to drama school."

Martha, as in Washington, America's first First Lady? Something clicked in Liam's brain, reminding him Dolley was a First Lady's name, too. Dolley Madison. "The dogs are named for First Ladies, like the sheep?"

"Martha was Brad and Brielle's pet before the sheep came along, but she gave me and Brielle the idea for the White House–inspired names. I don't know enough about Mrs. Washington to say if they have traits in common, but Martha's a loyal buddy and a good judge of character."

His head swiveled up. "I pass the Martha test, then?"

"I guess so." Her cheeks pinking, she looked away. "Come meet everyone. Can I get you a cup of coffee?"

"Sure. Thanks." One last pat on the dog's tummy, and he rose to greet the others. He knew a few. Gretchen Weinbach, of course, and Kellan Lambert was Grandma's next-door neighbor, so he saw him almost daily. Kellan's grandma Eileen perched on the loveseat beside Grandma's friend Trudie, who turned out to be the great aunt of Kellan's wife, Paige. He'd forgotten how small a town Widow's Peak Creek was.

However, he had no recollection of Faith Santos from his school days when she'd been Faith Latham. She looked younger, though, so they probably hadn't over-lapped classes.

He sat on one end of the plush white couch, across from Grandma's friends. "What are you two tasked with?"

"A little of everything, you could say. Some elements of the fair last all weekend, like the historical reenact-ments, Kellan's book fair, musical acts and the 'adven-ture' area Gretchen is setting up with carnival games and bounce houses, activities like that. Other things are one-time events, and the two of us oversee the art fair and the children's pet show, which both take place on the Saturday of the festival." Trudie pushed her long silver-streaked hair over her shoulder.

"I heard about the pet show from my grandma, but I don't understand. Is it like a beauty pageant?"

"Oh, no, more like a parade in reverse. The kids will be stationed behind tables in the exhibition hall, show-ing off their pets to the visitors who walk through. Ev-eryone gets a prize for participating and will hopefully boost his or her confidence."

Sounded sweet. "I can imagine it'll be a blast."

"I'm also in charge of the first aid station. I was a nurse back in the day." Eileen pushed her gold-rimmed glasses farther up her nose. "We heard from Marigold you're helping Clementine with two Saturday events, the vendor fair and cooking contest."

"That's right, but I don't know any details. Is the recipe contest a typical chili cook-off?"

"Not quite. Clementine came up with something different." Trudie leaned forward. "Gold foods for Gold Rush Days. 'Gold Star Favorites.'"

Gretchen sat beside him on a houndstooth-patterned wingback chair. "It's corny, but it sticks with the theme."

Cheeks flushing, Clementine set a full mug of coffee on the table before Liam. "Chili cook-offs are fun, but not everyone has a chili recipe. Most people can make something featuring a yellow or orange ingredient, though. Apricots, cornbread, squash. Anything similar in color will do. The only rule is we don't allow real gold. You know how some restaurants shave gold onto chocolate cake? That sort of thing is too expensive for everyone to do, and this is supposed to be fun for the whole town."

He'd never had such shavings on anything, but he'd take her word for it. Gretchen put an end to the conversation by tapping her pen against her purple plastic clipboard and calling the meeting to order.

Clementine slipped onto the couch beside him, the only available seat left. If sitting close to him bugged her, she didn't let on, although she didn't so much as glance at him. She stared at the notebook on her lap.

Gretchen might be the queen bee when it came to the festival, but it didn't take long to figure out Faith Santos was the heart of the operation. Part of the point of the festival was to educate folks about the town's history, and that was her area of expertise. He learned the newlywed ran an antiques store and had spearheaded the grand opening of a town museum a few weeks ago. Her plans to show guests what life was like in Widow's Peak Creek during the 1850s sounded fun. Interpreters would assist visitors in panning for gold, using a spinning wheel and laundering clothes in a washtub, among other things.

There would also be food trucks, snack booths, a bluegrass concert Saturday night, two opportunities for Mayor Judy Hughes to address the crowds, and a quilt show and flower show on the Sunday of the festival.

For over an hour, they segmented a map of the fairgrounds for each of the festival's activities and discussed ticket sales, security and publicity—or lack thereof, as it turned out. Flyers had been hanging around town for a few weeks, and there had been newspaper ads, but they seemed to have run their course. Liam pulled out his phone and searched online for the festival's social media presence. "You've announced the proceeds go to charity?"

"It's in the ads, the flyers and on our social media page that all ticket proceeds go to the town historic preservation fund," Faith said. "We're asking vendors to donate a percentage of their earnings to the fund, however, instead of a flat fee."

Sounded good. "Other than print ads, are you running any commercials?"

"We discussed it initially, but they're out of budget." Clementine cradled her coffee. "The mayor wants to bring in tourism, but she's not a huge fan of historical-based events, so the town council didn't make a donation to the cause."

"Maybe we can try some new approaches, then." He held up his phone, revealing the festival's website. "The site looks good, but if you're interested in adding new content, I'd be happy to film some stuff for it. Nature shots, someone panning for gold, things like that. And even if we can't buy commercials, it couldn't hurt to call KWPC. They might be interested in interviewing someone about the festival." The local radio station was always chatting with guests during the morning and evening commute hours. They used to, at any rate.

"Great ideas, Liam." Clementine jotted notes. "Gretchen, as our leader, would you be willing to talk to the radio?"

Their leader's hand went to her throat. "Me? I'm so shy, but for the cause, of course."

Shy? Liam and Clementine exchanged amused glances. Then she looked away, her gaze landing on the mantel clock. Her lips parted. "It's later than I thought. You all are welcome to stay and chat, but I have to get Annie from preschool."

"I think we're finished, and I have to be back at work anyway." Gretchen shoved her clipboard into a quilted blue bag.

Faith's eyes grew wide. "The time got away from me, too. There's a museum board meeting in half an hour."

"I should get back to the store." Kellan pulled a key ring from his jeans pocket. "Ready, ladies?"

"He's our ride back to Creekside Retirement Village," Trudie said to Liam.

"You all have a good rest of the day." Liam wasn't in a hurry, so he would help clean up before heading out. He hooked a finger through the handles of his and Gretchen's empty mugs and carried them to the kitchen.

Clementine waved her hand. "Thanks, Liam, but it's all right. I'll get to the dishes when I come back."

He wouldn't keep her, then. Following the others, he

made his way to his car, which he'd parked in full sun. Oven-hot air rolled over him when he opened the door. Ugh. He'd have to invest in a sunshade for the rental. And remember to crack the windows.

The others were in greater hurries than he was, and if he tried to leave first, he'd block their exit by making a three-point turn out of her driveway. Might as well sit for a minute. He lowered the automatic windows to let in the breeze, waving at the others as they drove past, including Clementine in her gold SUV. Too bad they hadn't had the opportunity to talk about divvying up their responsibilities for the festival. He could call later and ask, except he didn't have her phone number.

Grandma surely would, and he could ask her.

His phone buzzed. Maybe Grandma needed something from the store. Nope, it was the producer from his latest project, Javier, inquiring into Liam's recovery.

You'd better get healed up, dude, because the Indonesia project might be a go and I want you on it.

Working with Javier had been a blast, so the thought of heading out with him again made him smile. Liam pecked out a reply with his right forefinger, lamenting his loss of texting with both thumbs, thanks to his injury.

Following doctor's orders so it should all be good. Can't wait.

Speaking of doctor's orders? His surgery site could use an ice pack right about now, and a dose of over-the-counter pain medication wouldn't be a bad idea, either. Good thing he was headed back to the tiny house—

Something moved on the north edge of Clementine's property. The distance was farther than the length of a football field away, but there was no mistaking a figure in blue, back hunched like it was burdened beneath a backpack, slinking along the fence before disappearing into the cottonwoods where Clementine had told him the small creek ended in a ponding basin.

The forward-bending, hobbled walk told Liam it had to be her next-door neighbor Fergus Campbell.

What was he doing on Clementine's property? Had Liam and Clementine's patch not held up? If that was the case... Oh, no. Had a sheep got out?

Throat tightening, Liam rushed from the car and crossed the driveway, scanning the fields to count the sheep. Dolley lazed in the shade, unconcerned, while six grown sheep nibbled the grass. Clementine had said she had six ewes, right? Eleanor and Frances and, oh boy, he couldn't remember the other names. But there were six.

Farther afield was a larger sheep that had to be the ram. So the adult sheep were accounted for, then, but what about the lambs? His racing mind couldn't dredge up the memory of how many babies there were.

Which meant he had no way to verify all the lambs were safe. And if Fergus was over by the ponding basin? Was he there because a lamb had got out and gone that way? Lambs couldn't swim, could they? Liam's stomach lurched.

The lambs were important to Clementine's livelihood, of course, but they were also precious to the family. Annie's sweet face had lit up when she told him about her and Wynn's plans to enter their lamb into the pet show at the festival.

He couldn't just stand here while something treasured to Clementine and her kids was in trouble.

"We painted bunnies to decorate the classroom for Easter." Annie continued the list of things she'd accomplished at preschool today. "My bunny is pink all over."

"Your favorite color." Smiling, Clementine pulled into her driveway. Her smile fell at seeing Liam's car still parked by the house, and then Liam himself, clambering over the picket fence's locked gate at the opposite end of the driveway. Why was he going toward the barn and fields?

He must have heard the car, though, because he looked up and turned around, then fluidly bounded back over the gate. With only one working arm, he still made it look easy. Once again, her mind went to how impressed she'd always been by his effortless-looking athletic ability—but this was not the time to indulge in those kinds of thoughts. Athletic prowess was not nearly as important as what he was doing hopping her fence.

Besides, wasn't her agenda to get him out of her system once and for all? If she admired him at all, it would have to be objectively. Nothing…personal.

Her priorities reestablished, she parked her car in front of the house and hopped out, hurrying to assist Annie from her car seat. By the time she was finished, Liam was within shouting distance. "What's up? Your car won't start?" And if so, why was he over there instead of calling for a tow truck?

He hitched his thumb behind him. "I think a sheep got out."

Impossible. Rex had checked the perimeter fence this morning and said it all looked good, even the patchwork job she and Liam made on Saturday. "Why do you say that?"

"Because Fergus just went to the ponding basin." Liam tipped his head back toward the northwest corner of her property. "Why else would he be there if he didn't see a lamb in need of a rescue? I think it's a lamb, anyway, because I counted seven adult sheep in the field, but I forgot how many lambs there are supposed to be."

"A lot," Annie said, spreading her arms wide. "It takes forever to feed them bottles."

"It sure seems like it, doesn't it?" Clementine stroked Annie's hair, affirming her contribution to the conversation, all while trying to wrap her mind around Liam's words. "The thing is, Liam, my animals can't get to the creek or the ponding basin. They're two fenced fields away right now, plus there's yet another fence blocking access to the water." She'd pledged with other farmers and ranchers to protect local water sources, but there was also the sheep's safety to consider...as well as the kids'. "The pond is deeper than it appears. After a bad flood year, Brad and Brielle had it dug lower so it holds more overflow."

"I understand why you're careful." He glanced at Annie. "But I'm not sure why else Fergus would be there."

Unlikely as it was that any of her animals were at the pond, she made a quick head count of the lambs. Fifteen. Just right. And Dolley sprawled in the shade, unaffected, but she never got worked up over Fergus. "That's so weird. He'd have to hop his fence to walk from his house along the creek. I can't imagine him— Oh."

"*Oh* what?"

"Last summer, kids climbed my western fence to

mess around at the pond." Just what she needed today, truants messing up her pond. "Maybe they're back. Fergus saw them and is chasing them off."

"I didn't see any kids, just him, but if they hopped the west fence, I guess that could explain why I couldn't see them. They're hidden from view." Liam's hand went to his sling in an unconscious-looking gesture.

He must be in pain to do that. She wouldn't keep him any longer. "I appreciate the heads-up. You can go home and ice that collarbone now. Come on, Annie, let's go to the creek before we eat lunch."

Annie skipped ahead, but to Clementine's surprise, Liam followed after her. "I'd like to come along in case Fergus found kids who are…belligerent." His voice was low, intended for her ears, not Annie's, even though Annie had started singing a song about a rabbit. "Let me back you up."

She'd been taking care of herself, two kids, and a farm for two years now, and she had no need of anyone's help, save God's. She certainly didn't need Liam's assistance, but the gesture was kind.

And truth be told, his presence was comforting. She didn't dare dwell on why, but right now, she decided not to fight it.

"All right." They walked to the gate he'd just hopped over, and Clementine opened it with her key. A few yards later, they entered the gate to the north paddock. The grass tickled her ankles as they strode to the last of the gates they had to get through, the one that separated them from Blue Creek and the ponding basin.

Annie started to run ahead to the creek, but Clementine took her hand to hold her back. If there were strange kids in there, she didn't want anything to happen to

Annie. She didn't want to scare Annie, though, so she gave her hand three squeezes, their family's code for *I-love-you*, and something she'd learned from her parents. "Stay close in case someone's here we don't know."

"But I don't see any people."

Clementine didn't either, but that didn't mean someone wasn't out of sight, in the trees. It was no use trying to surprise anyone, as noisy as they were being, so she might as well flush possible interlopers out. "Hello?"

With a muffled grunt, a figure emerged from the cottonwoods. Fergus, just as Liam had said, with a worn backpack over his shoulders and a more pronounced totter to his walk than usual. He generally looked unhappy to see her, but right now, a scowl deepened the wrinkles on his cheeks. "Give a man a heart attack, sneaking up on him like that."

"Sorry, Fergus, but what's going on?" She curved around the trees to get a good look at the ponding basin. No more than twenty by thirty feet, the reed-and-grass lined water was smooth as a mirror. "Did you see kids trespassing? A few broke into the ponding basin last summer."

"Yep, I did." Fergus swiped his nose with the side of one gnarled hand. "Good-for-nothing slackers, splashing and making a ruckus. Rushed off when they saw me."

"Can I splash, too?" Annie frowned when Clementine shook her head in response.

Liam rubbed the back of his neck. "I didn't hear anything. Dolley didn't indicate she did, either."

"She doesn't bark at most people," Clementine reminded him, although Dolley normally alerted her with a whine or tense stance when something unusual was afoot. Maybe she wasn't concerned by the trespassers because they were so far from the sheep.

Liam circled behind Fergus. "Looks like you got a little wet. You all right?"

Now that Liam mentioned it, Fergus's jeans were wet from the knees down. His jacket sported damp blotches. She rushed toward him while Liam rounded the pond and inspected the fence. "Did you fall in? Are you okay?"

"Bah." Fergus waved her away. "My knees aren't what they used to be, and they give out sometimes, not that it's your business. You're welcome, by the way."

Oops. She hadn't thanked him fast enough. It seemed she was always making a bad impression on Fergus. "Thank you. How many kids were there, do you know?"

"I didn't stop to count them, missy." His glower deepened. "Thought it would be more important to run them off."

"What'd they look like?" Liam's brow furrowed.

"I didn't get a good look while I was chasing them off." Fergus straightened the straps of his faded blue backpack over his shoulders. "I'm getting a mite weary intervening over here. You aren't gonna like hearin' this, missy, but this farm is too much for you."

His words hit her hard, like she'd been headbutted by Scooter, the ram. But she was no softie, and when she was hit, she got right back up. "You don't know me well, but I take good care of this place and my animals. Everything's fine."

Except…it wasn't, was it? Eleanor had got out and now truants hopped her fence. Okay, so things were in a rough patch, but that didn't mean she couldn't handle her farm. "It won't be long now before I install electric fencing."

His eyebrows rose, but then his hands fisted on his narrow hips. "Seems too little too late, if you ask me. Nice land, though. If you decide to sell, talk to me first."

She glanced at Annie. The little girl had wandered a few feet up Blue Creek and seemed more interested in rock hunting, but that didn't mean she wasn't listening. "I'm not selling Honeysuckle Farm."

"I said *if.*"

"Never." This was the kids' home. The place where their parents had planned to raise them. She could never take them away from here.

"If you see sense, you know where to find me." Walking off in that forward-bent way of his, Fergus glanced at Annie, whose arm was elbow deep in the shallow creek.

Clementine rubbed her aching temple. "Annie, no playing in the water today."

"I'm not playing, Clemmie. I'm collecting. See? Another one." She held up a reddish-brown rock, its watery shine making it look like a polished gemstone.

"Another for your collection." Clementine gave a thumbs-up at the latest addition, but frustration gnawed at her insides. "Let's take it back to the house. There's a lot to do."

Liam gestured at the fence line. "It doesn't look like the kids messed up the fence."

It looked okay to her, too. "I meant the barn, actually. There's a leak over my milking stanchion, and I'm not sure how bad the problem is. I have to get on the roof and see what's going on." Not that she relished the idea. The leak was coming from the highest section of the roof. She prayed she could see the problem from the relative safety of her ten-foot ladder so she wouldn't have to crawl onto one of the sloped lower sections of roof. She needed to see the extent of the problem and plan her budget accordingly.

Her stomach pinched. Expenses and heights, two fear-inducing things. She never used to worry about money, but that was before she had a farm and two kids to support. Things had been so tight, she hadn't been able to sock anything away for the kids' futures, which caused her some concern.

Nor did she used to be afraid of climbing trees or ladders, but since Brielle and Brad died, anything that could possibly lead to injury made her nervous. If she slipped off the ladder, the kids would be alone—

Stop thinking the worst. God's with me. He'll give me strength to do what needs to be done.

Liam touched Clementine's elbow so lightly it almost felt like the stir of the breeze, but it was enough to tug her from her panicky thoughts.

His eyes were wide and dark. "Hey, I said I'd help you out, remember?"

It took a minute to find her tongue. "With the festival, yes."

"Grandma was right. I'm used to being busy, and it just so happens I have a lot of time on my hands. So if it's festivals or fences, teenage delinquents, pushy neighbors, whatever. I'm here to help. You might have to show me how to shear a sheep or something."

He was trying to be funny, so she made a show of rolling her eyes. "You're off the hook there. They were shorn before they had their babies."

"Phew. Because even with two hands, I can barely give a buddy a haircut when we're off filming."

Annie looked at him like he needed some educating. "Sheep don't have hair, silly. They have wool."

"A wool-cut, then." Liam moved his hand a few inches over Annie's head, buzzing like an electric razor. "Oops, sorry, Annie. Now you have a sheep hairdo."

Giggling, Annie ran ahead, clutching her dark blond ponytail like it was in danger of falling off.

Clementine appreciated Liam's offer, but the last thing she wanted to do was put anyone out on her account. "It's not necessary, honest. Fergus may be right about some things, but I'm not in that bad of shape."

"I want to help because I'm able and have time to do it, not because I'm listening to Fergus. I don't like how he talks to you, though."

She waved it off. "He's vexing, but I can't blame him for being irritated that my fence doesn't hold up. Or for wanting my farm. He knows a jewel when he sees it."

"Why'd he have a backpack?"

"He said he was checking his fence, didn't he? It's probably easier for him to carry tools in a pack than a box." It didn't much matter, considering everything else on her mind right now. It felt as if her to-do list was insurmountable. And here was Liam, offering to help with farm repairs.

But she wanted closure when it came to him, not to be around him more.

Maybe she was looking at this all wrong. Maybe spending time with Liam was the way she'd finally gain finality in their relationship. They'd have time to talk.

Or maybe she was just so overwhelmed she couldn't think straight, but she realized she was nodding.

"Okay, Liam."

"Okay?" Why did he have to grin like an eager schoolboy?

"Before we look at the roof, though, we need lunch. It's past noon."

"Peanut butter and honey." Annie informed, rather than requested, her preference.

Peanut butter and honey were just Clementine's speed today, though. "Care to stay?"

"Oh yeah. I love peanut butter and honey."

"You can sit by me." Annie tugged his hand. "And eat from one of my princess plates."

His grin widened, like there was nothing on earth he wanted more than to sit with a four-year-old and eat off her toddler-safe plates.

It was sweet and frankly so attractive Clementine's heart swelled to twice its size. *God, if the plan is for me to put Liam firmly in the past, I'm going to need Your help.*

She'd need His guidance to gain closure, because while she'd grown accustomed to the absence of Liam in her life, that didn't mean her heart wasn't in danger of breaking all over again when he left in a few weeks.

Chapter Four

After Clementine rinsed the lunch plates—one plain white and two decorated with cartoon princesses—she got Annie settled on the patio with her toy cars. As Martha stretched out beside the little girl for a rest, Clementine led Liam inside the barn to show him where she'd first become aware of the leak. "I was milking, and then splat." She pointed at the ceiling.

"No water staining below or above, which is good, of course." He turned his gaze from the ceiling and floor to his surroundings, taking in the workbench, supplies and tools, and straw-filled pens. "The sheep sleep in here at night?"

"They're free to come and go as they please. The ewes come in here to be milked twice a day, and they have their babies in the security of the pens, but if they want protection from rain, they tend to congregate in the open-air shelter outside. Anyway, there's another floor above this section of barn, so there might be more evidence of the leak upstairs. Come on up."

"Lead the way." He followed her up the creaking stairs to the storage loft. There, they stood among bags of feed and storage boxes, staring at the timber ceiling. Liam shook his head. "I don't see a damp spot."

Clementine crouched and patted the dusty floorboards. "The floor's dry, too. I'm relieved, but I was hoping for a clue as to where the leak originated so I know where to look when I'm up there."

"At least we have a general area." Liam walked in a circle, staring up. "I saw a ladder propped against the wall downstairs. Is that the tallest one you have?"

"Yep." And knowing she'd have to climb it soon made her skin slither.

"Before you get on the roof, do you want to call the police about the kids in the ponding basin? I can keep an eye on Annie."

Oh, right. Clementine's fear of heights had run all thought of the trespassers from her mind. "I'm not sure I need to involve the police. The kids didn't do any damage."

"They didn't get the chance. It might be good to have a report on file in case they come back again, though. It's warm enough to be swimming weather."

She made a face. "I wouldn't want to jump in that water. It's murky and fishy."

"Fish?" He followed her back down the stairs, his boots thudding loud behind her. "They might not want to swim, then, but catch fish."

"I doubt it, not when there are so many better options around here. I mean, Widow's Peak Creek has several species, but you won't find much in my pond beyond mosquito fish, courtesy of local vector control." At the bottom of the stairs, she turned to wait for him. "If kids hop the fence again, I'll call the police, okay? In the meantime, I'll keep a closer eye on things. Clearly,

I've been slacking on the job, letting things slip. Like the fence and the roof."

"Things wear out, Clementine. That doesn't mean you're not doing your part. We all do the best we can with what we have, right?" He cupped her upper arm in a supportive gesture.

It was hard to think with him so close, his hand so warm and comforting on her arm. She moved away before she lost all sense. "Right. Thanks for the reminder."

Before she fully registered what he was doing, he moved to the ladder and hefted it in his right arm. "All right, let's get you on the roof." He marched outside.

She ran after him. "You just had surgery. You shouldn't be carrying that."

"I can't let my right arm atrophy while the left side heals."

"You shouldn't push it, either."

"I'm not." He paused outside the northernmost wing of the barn by a flat stretch of dirt. "Is this where you want it? Seems like it's as close as we can get to the spot where you felt the leak."

"Perfect." She turned to check on Annie. Her niece played contentedly, making *vroom* noises and driving one of the toy cars around Martha's paws. Ever patient, Martha lay still, except for her tail, which flicked in a happy motion.

It was important to Clementine for the kids to always know where to find her, so she waved. "We're over here now, Annie."

"Okay, Clemmie," Annie called, not looking up.

Liam gave the ladder one final adjustment. "Huh."

"What?" Was something wrong with the ladder?

Besides the fact that it was a million years old and splotched with paint spatter?

"It just dawned on me. The kids don't call you *aunt*."

Oh, that. "Annie was only two when we lost Brielle and Brad. After a little while, she started calling me Mommy, which upset Wynn. It was hard for me to hear, too, but Annie was practically a baby. She wanted stability, permanence. Anyway, we decided to merge Clementine and Mommy together. Clemmie." The name was as natural to her now as the one on her birth certificate.

"That must have been such a hard time for all of you. Grieving, adjusting. I mean, you had to take on a farm."

She took a step back to eye the ladder's position. "It helped that I was already living here when Brielle and Brad died. I'd been downsized—I was writing copy for an advertiser—so I decided to take advantage of the opportunity to switch to agricultural-related journalism. I was scheduled to start an out-of-state internship that summer, but in the interim, Brad and Brielle invited me to live with them. That's how I learned the routine with the sheep and the kids."

"You never did the internship, did you?" His voice sounded sad.

"I couldn't take the kids away from everything familiar to them." Too many well-meaning people had encouraged her to "put herself first" to follow her dream, but the cost of uprooting Wynn and Annie was too high, in Clementine's view.

She expected a similar sentiment to come from Liam, but instead, he looked thoughtful. "You're right. Kids need a sense of security. Not just physical but emotional."

With a flash of memory, she recalled that emotional security was something his parents hadn't always provided. She'd always envied him having Marigold as a grandma, but his home life hadn't been peaceful. Recalling his dad's flakiness and his mom's anger and then his dad's short, fatal illness, her heart broke for him all over again.

Until this moment, she hadn't realized he could have been recuperating with his mother, Barbara, but instead he'd chosen to visit Marigold. In fact, he hadn't even mentioned his mother. Marigold still exchanged Christmas cards with Barb and, in January, had mentioned Barb lived in Nevada and seemed in good health. Why was Liam here for six weeks instead of with his mom? This didn't seem like the right time to ask.

Besides, she had to get on the roof. She couldn't ask Rex to help her with this sort of thing, not with his arthritis, so she had to do this herself. Might as well get it over with.

Fear filled her belly like liquid that spread through her arteries and dampened her hands. Wiping her palms on her jean-clad thighs, she glanced at Liam. "Hold it steady for me?"

"Sure." He braced it with his right arm.

She scaled the first five rungs and made the mistake of looking back at Annie. Uh-oh. Wooziness crashed over her like a white-capped wave.

It must have shown because Liam shifted below her. "You okay?"

"Yep." It came out through gritted teeth.

"I take it you're not comfortable on the ladder."

Comfortable? Ha. She was petrified, but she slowly made it to the next rung, praying all the while. "I don't like heights."

"I don't remember that at all. In fact, I remember us

being stuck at the top of the Ferris wheel at the county fair for forty-five minutes and laughing about it. Hanging over the edge and—"

"Can we not discuss this right now?" Her hands were slick with sweat and her ankles were wobbling. *You're with me, God. You're with me.*

"Tell you what. Come down and let someone else do this."

"I'm not asking Rex. He'd do it, but he'd be in so much pain with his arthritis—"

"I meant me. Hold the ladder, and I'll climb up there."

She didn't dare look down at him, else she become even woozier. "In case you forgot, you only have use of one arm."

"One arm is all it takes."

"Are you sure?" Her voice was a squeak.

"I'm the guy who couldn't stay out of trees, remember? Now I get paid to rappel down cliffs. Come on down."

All right, then. It took her half the time to get down as it had to get up, but even back on solid ground, her ankles still wobbled. "Thanks, Liam."

He scaled the ladder in about three seconds. While she willed her erratic pulse to return to normal, he paused on the second-to-top rung, his upper body leaning against the side of the barn since the ladder didn't reach all the way. He peeked down at her, grimacing. "The gutters could use a good clean out."

One more thing for the to-do list. She was about to comment when he winked and clambered atop the roof, disappearing from sight.

Her stomach flipped, and she wasn't even the one on the roof. "Be careful up there."

He yelled down something affirmative.

Clearly, traipsing over a slanted surface more than a story high might not be a big deal to Liam, but it was to Clementine. She had to be careful in everything she did, to ensure a reckless accident didn't part Wynn and Annie from the only parent figure they had. Liam had no idea what sort of gift he was giving to her right now, taking her place.

Lord, please protect him up there.

Her lips parted. That was the first prayer she'd offered on Liam's behalf in years. She used to pray for him daily when they were together. For his family. For his faith or, back then, lack of it. She'd stopped when she ended their relationship, but maybe she shouldn't have. Had anyone, other than Marigold, prayed for him these past sixteen years?

Liam returned to the roof's edge, peering down at her. "Good news and bad news."

Oh boy. "Yeah?"

"The good news is I can't see any damaged roof tiles that would allow water to leak in."

"That's the bad news, too, isn't it? You can't tell where the damage is."

His apologetic nod confirmed it. "The problem has to be on the second-story roof, directly above the storage loft, but I can't get up there today. It'll take more than this ladder, for starters."

Did that mean a costlier repair job? The electric fencing options she'd been eying would have to wait, although she did have an opportunity to make a good amount selling soaps at the festival vendor fair. "Thanks. I'll let the roofer know when I call them."

"I can probably make the repairs, but why don't I

come down so we can talk instead of shouting about it?" He sat on the roof edge.

Clementine renewed her grip on the ladder so it would be steady when his foot found purchase on the top rung. Behind her, she could hear the squealing brakes of Wynn's school bus, followed by the hydraulic hiss of the door opening at the end of the driveway. She glanced over her shoulder to watch Wynn exit the bus. She was always so happy to see him at the end of the school day.

A scraping sound from above drew her attention back up. Liam had twisted around to descend the ladder, but his foot must have slipped off the top rung because he balanced on his stomach, his feet tapping in search of the ladder rungs. He was off by a few inches.

"Liam! To the left." The words came out clear and loud, despite fear constricting her throat. In under a second, a prickly-sick tingling sensation flooded her limbs. Her chest tightened, making it difficult to breathe. All too well, she recognized the start of a panic attack.

"Hold on." Her words were as much for him as for herself. She had no choice but to climb up after him and guide his feet to the rungs. *Lord, help me do this. And oh, please, don't let him fall in front of the kids.*

The toe of Liam's boot grazed the ladder, and with a slight shimmy to the left, just as Clementine directed, he found the rung. When both feet were planted safely, he released his light hold of the vent he'd grabbed—it wouldn't have held his weight for long if he'd been unable to find the ladder and slipped, but since he'd been centered on his stomach, he could've found another handhold. No problem.

Once both feet were squared away on rungs, he descended. And almost stepped on Clementine's hand. "Oops. I didn't see you climbing up after me."

On the ground, she skittered back, giving him room to step down. "I was going to grab your boot. Guide you to the ladder."

"Thanks, Clementine. I didn't even think about that option. I free climb enough that I'm pretty good at anchoring myself by my fingertips if I have to— Hey, are you okay?"

"Fine." But her fingers shook, and her eyes had a glazed look to them. Then she turned away to greet Wynn. Liam hadn't heard the boy come home from school, but there he was, backpack over his shoulders, stepping into Clementine's hug.

"Hey buddy, how was your day?" Her tone was peppy, but her fingers still trembled.

"Good. Whatcha doing?"

"Inspecting the roof for the source of a leak."

Annie ran to the ladder, Martha lumbering after her. "Can I go up?"

"No," Wynn and Clementine said at the same time.

Clementine shifted the ladder away from Annie, like she was preparing to return it to the barn. "It's extremely dangerous, even for grown-ups. Don't ever climb the ladder, okay, guys?"

"I won't, ever," Wynn promised.

"Okay." Annie rubbed her stomach. "Is it snack time?"

"Sure is. Go inside and wash up. Bananas and peanut butter pretzels are on the counter. I'll be inside in a minute." Clementine's smile had a strained quality to it.

Liam grabbed the ladder and carried it to the barn.

Clementine followed him. "Thanks for your help. I

appreciate you sticking around when I'm sure your injury needs attention."

An ice pack would feel mighty good about now, but he had the distinct feeling she was rushing him off. She was clearly upset. About what, though, he hadn't a clue. She didn't like heights anymore, but she was safe on the ground now. What was the problem?

"What's going on? You've seemed upset since I came down from the roof."

"Of course I'm upset. You almost fell. You could've broken your neck as well as your collarbone."

"I wouldn't have fallen that far. I'd have been okay."

"Maybe. That's a big thing to risk in front of Wynn and Annie, don't you think?"

It hadn't seemed like that big of a threat to him. Frankly, it still didn't. He climbed all the time and had experienced his share of falls.

Then her words about Wynn and Annie hit him like a fist in the solar plexus. *Risk.* Was this about Brielle and Brad? The kids' parents died while skiing. An area with a more challenging descent had been closed off due to avalanche danger. Despite warning signs, they chose to try the slope. Surely on that otherwise normal day, the possibility of an avalanche had seemed miniscule. Farfetched, the sort of thing that happened only in movies.

But the worst had happened that day, and Clementine was left to pick up the pieces. If she were overly cautious now, could he blame her?

He hadn't meant to upset her, but he could see where she was coming from. "I didn't think about how it must have looked, with my feet missing the ladder or how you could perceive it. I'd never want to scare the kids.

Or you." But he had. "I'm so sorry, Clementine. Is it all right for me to apologize to the kids?"

Her features crumpled, from anger to something akin to sorrow. "That's not necessary. I don't even think they saw it and… I shouldn't have snapped at you like that. It's no excuse, but if there's a threat to the kids or even the possibility something could happen in their line of sight, my brain goes to freak-out mode. Teens hopping my fence to get into my ponding basin? Not a problem. But heights, stuff like that? I should've expected a panic attack at the prospect of going on the roof, but I thought it was under control. Clearly not. I went full-on fight-or-flight. I know terror is not the healthiest reaction, and believe me, I've been working on it. Pastor Benton says—well, it doesn't matter right now. I'm just sorry I spoke to you so harshly."

Panic attack? This was going from bad to worse. He wasn't sure what such a reaction was supposed to look like, but if Clementine said she was experiencing one, he believed her. "How can I help?"

"You can't, honest. I have to get through it. Remind myself God is in control." She exited the barn, arms wrapped around herself, breathing deeply.

Regret pooled in Liam's stomach. "I caused this, and if there's something I can do to fix it, I want to."

"You didn't cause it. You didn't try to miss the rung." She puffed out a ragged breath. "I'm sorry I'm even telling you all of this, but honest, it's not on you. You couldn't have known."

He got it. Really. He couldn't have known. But maybe he *should* have perceived more was going on with her than a recently acquired fear of heights.

That was the problem, wasn't it? No matter how

much he'd always wanted to be there for Clementine, he was unaware of what she needed.

Following her up the porch steps, he felt seventeen again, exactly as he had the night before his mom moved him and his sister to southern California. He'd arrived at her house sad, but certain their long-distance relationship would be a temporary thing. Once he graduated from high school, they could be together again. Nothing as insignificant as miles could damage a love like theirs.

He'd been wrong, of course. That night, she'd said she wanted to make a clean break.

He hadn't been worth waiting for. He'd been lacking in her eyes.

He still was. Nothing for it but to head back to the tiny house and leave her be.

The screech of the screen door pulled him around. The kids strode onto the porch, half-eaten bananas in hand. Thankfully, they didn't look too traumatized by his near fall.

Annie twirled her banana, like the peel was a skirt on a doll. "Can we have popsicles, Clemmie?"

"Sure." Clementine's voice still sounded strained, but she did a good job hiding her anxiety from the kids.

"Mr. Liam, do you want one?" Wynn's smile was shy. "They're orange juice and mango."

"They sound great, but I need to get back to my grandma's. Ice my collarbone."

"Does ice fix it?" Wynn's eyes narrowed.

"It helps." Liam glanced at Clementine. "If it's okay, I'll get your number from Grandma and text you. Then you can send me a list of things to do for the festival. At your convenience."

She made a tutting noise. "We didn't even talk about it, did we?"

"You can talk about it over a popsicle," Wynn suggested.

"I think Mr. Liam needs to get home, Wynn, but you've inspired me. We should have Liam to dinner one night and talk about the festival." Clementine's smile looked more authentic now. "Marigold's welcome, too. Does Friday work?"

"I'll bring dessert."

For the second time, he waved goodbye and got into his car. Despite his leaving the windows cracked open, it was still hot enough to bake a pizza on the dashboard. Liam started the ignition to get the AC going but didn't drive off.

How could he? The pain in his gut was ten times worse than his throbbing collarbone. Clementine was struggling, and even if she allowed him to help, there wasn't much he could do, could he? Except pray.

Which he did, right there in the sweltering car. For peace to prevail in her heart and mind, for healing, for… He didn't even know what to pray, but God knew what was best for Clementine.

As he drove away from Honeysuckle Farm, he determined to keep praying for her in the coming days. Weeks. Years, if necessary. Ironic, since he'd spent the last sixteen years trying to banish her from his mind.

But something had shifted inside him today. Her well-being was more important than the lingering pangs of his teenage heartache.

If he'd really loved her once, it seemed like the least he could do.

Chapter Five

While getting up early was part of Liam's routine, he was not a morning person, and he was bleary-eyed when he walked into the back room of Del's Café at 6:00 a.m. Wednesday morning. Good thing he was in the company of the three things that could get his day off to a good start. The Lord, fellowship and a mug filled to the brim with steaming hot coffee.

"Milk or sugar?" The man around his age seated at the table beside him was built like a linebacker, so the tiny cream pitcher looked comically like a doll's toy in his huge hand.

"No, thanks. I like my coffee black." Liam took a long pull from his cup and felt the warmth go down to his stomach. "I'm starting to feel more human already."

"I hear that, Liam." The guy offered his hand. "Joel Morgan."

Grandma had mentioned him, a lawyer who had helped Clementine with the legal aspects of her guardianship. "Nice to meet you, but it sounds like you know who I am."

"It's not that big of a town," Joel joked. "You're Marigold's grandson, Clementine Simon's—"

"Helper, with the Gold Rush Days festival," Liam offered before Joel could say something else. Like how Liam was Clementine's high school boyfriend.

The church's pastor, Benton Hunt, was on Liam's other side. Dropping a sugar cube into his coffee, he glanced at Liam. "How is it going, being back in town after so long?"

Was that a dig about Liam not visiting Grandma more often? Then he saw a sincere kinship in Benton's eyes, and Liam realized he'd meant something different altogether. "I'd forgotten that you moved away from Widow's Peak Creek as a teenager, too." Liam took another sip of coffee. "It's good. Some things have changed, and some things have stayed the same."

"Like what?" Joel picked up a laminated menu. "I'm a newer addition to town, so I'm always interested in hearing others' impressions."

Joel probably referred to things like buildings or the townspeople, but all Liam could think about was Clementine. How she'd changed. She was more cautious, more determined in her convictions. But her beauty, her kindness, her love for her family? None of that had altered.

Stop thinking about Clementine all the time. You're not seventeen anymore.

Scrambling for examples that didn't have to do with his teenage relationship, he fiddled with his mug. "It's sad the old schoolhouse at the end of Main Street burned down. Grandma tells me there's a lot of work underway to preserve the town's other historic sites, though, including the new museum inside Hughes House. I heard you had something to do with that, Benton."

He'd learned from Grandma that Benton and his new fiancée, Leah, were responsible for turning the historic mansion into a town museum.

"Leah and I had a blast getting it fixed up before Christmas." Benton's eyes crinkled with his smile. "Once we're married, we'll live in the old servants' house behind the museum. It needs a lot of updating, but we're excited to put our own stamp on it."

"What's stayed the same in town?" Joel leaned back.

"The creek. My grandma's strong will," Liam teased. "The good people who live here."

Joel tapped the side of his mug with a fingernail. "It's a good place to raise Maisie. My daughter," he explained to Liam. "Well, stepdaughter. Marrying my late wife was a package deal. You may have known her. Adriana Davis."

Late? "I remember her from school, yeah. I'm sorry for your loss."

"Thanks, but like I said, the people here have been a blessing." He reached for his menu, closing the subject. "What kind of breakfast guy are you, Liam? If you prefer sausage to bacon, they have some locally made links here that are so spicy they'll singe off your taste buds."

The rest of the hour was spent eating, sharing and studying God's word. After the closing prayer, Liam looked around at the group of a dozen or so men ages twenty-five to eighty-four, some he knew, like Kellan, others he recognized, like Faith's husband, Tom Santos, and new acquaintances, like Joel.

They were all good guys. He had friends, of course, and had plenty of fun and good conversation with the various film crews he worked with, but this was different. The men here seemed to have formed long-lasting bonds with one another based on faith, friendship and a strong sense of community. They shared life together.

Liam hadn't shared life like that with anyone in a long, long time. And until now, he hadn't realized how much he'd missed it.

Clementine's week was fuller than usual. In addition to her regular tasks with the sheep, she had a lot to do in the soap shed while Annie was at preschool. Her product took a month or more to cure, so she'd planned ahead for the Gold Rush Days vendor fair, preparing extra batches of fragrant soap weeks ago.

Now that they'd cured, she carefully sliced each batch into over a hundred bars and wrapped the individual items in paper, sealing them with stickers she'd had printed up, featuring Lady Bird's adorable, pink-nosed face. Other wool products she'd created to sell, like dryer balls and dish scrubbies, went into sheer, decorative bags, along with her business card. By the end of the week, every flat surface in the soap shed was stacked with boxes of product. She had no idea how well she'd do at the festival compared to her average farmers' market sales, but she didn't want to be caught shorthanded.

Hopefully, she'd earn enough to afford the electric fencing outright. No more school-skipping teenagers would climb into her yard after that, at least, not painlessly. And the roof?

Every time it crossed her mind, she thought of Liam, which brought up a jumble of messy emotions. She had a lot to pray about, but she couldn't help wondering how things would be between them on Friday when he came over for dinner. She'd hoped Marigold would be there and provide a buffer between them, but Liam had texted to tell her his grandma had plans.

Why had she invited him to dinner? She could've met him at Angel Food Bakery or Del's Café to split up the festival to-do list while the kids were in school. Their meetup would have been short.

But also public. That's why she'd invited him over, so they wouldn't be subject to prying eyes and gossip. But the prospect of spending time with him made her so nervous by Friday evening that it was no wonder she jumped out of her skin when Liam rang the doorbell.

If he felt as awkward as she did about coming to dinner, it was hard to tell, because the kids and Martha were all over him the moment he walked in the front door. Annie twirled in a circle, Martha wagged her tail, and Wynn, her quiet boy, patted Liam's arm to get his full attention. She'd never seen him seek a person's attention like that before.

"Look at my new shoes, Mr. Liam."

"Those are sharp." Liam's eyes widened in approval at Wynn's leather ankle boots. "They're similar to mine."

Wynn's smiling cheeks were rosy apples. "Yep."

Clementine appreciated Liam's enthusiasm as he asked to see the tread. At the shoe store, it hadn't taken a genius to figure out Wynn wanted miniature replicas of Liam's shoes.

Annie tapped the white cardboard box Liam held. "What's that?"

Clementine hid her smirk behind her hand. Annie might not be able to read yet, but she'd been able to recognize the logo for Angel Food Bakery since she was a toddler. A bakery box equaled treats, plain and simple.

"I told your aunt I'd bring dessert. If it's okay with her, you can have some after you eat all of your dinner." He sniffed, nose in the air like a basset hound's. "It smells amazing, whatever it is."

"Chicken enchiladas." Clementine took the box from him. "I hope you still like them."

"Are you kidding? I'm surprised the kids like them, though."

"They're a favorite around here. Wynn is a green-chile aficionado, and Annie likes anything with tortillas."

"Quesadillas are my fav'rite." Annie rubbed a huge circle over her stomach.

"Plain cheese, or do you like anything else in there?"

Clementine left them to set down the box and get the enchiladas out of the oven. In a few minutes, they were all seated around the dining table set between the family room and the kitchen in the open floor plan. The conversation about quesadillas was still going on when Clementine served up the main dish, rice and salad, pausing only to say grace.

To Clementine's relief, Liam didn't seem the least bit uncomfortable or strained. He and the kids engaged well, and the sense of natural ease continued throughout a number of dinner topics, from the kids now being on spring break to the discovery of gold in the county back in the 1850s, which Wynn was learning about in school. There was never a spare second for conversation to grow awkward or stilted.

After everyone had their fill, Clementine set the box from Angel Food Bakery on the table. Wynn's eyes grew round as quarters. "What's inside?"

"Cookies." For the first time since arriving, Liam looked uncertain. "Something for everyone, I hope."

"I'll say." While the kids found their favorite iced cookies, Clementine selected a chocolate-covered macaroon. "Leah Dean told me these are her favorites. I've never tried them, though." One bite, and the silky chocolate and sticky-sweet coconut melted in her mouth. She gave a thumbs-up. "I can see why. These could be addictive."

"They can't be that good." A teasing glint flashed in Liam's eyes as he sampled one. Then his eyes shut. "Okay, they are."

Clementine rose from the table. "Please keep enjoying dessert, Liam. I'll just clear a few dishes, and then we can talk about the festival."

"I'm finished. What can I do?"

"Not a thing. Everything goes in the dishwasher." She'd even milked the ewes a little early so they could get straight to work. Thankfully, the last of the lambs had weaned from the bottle earlier this week.

The kids were young enough that she didn't ask them to do much in the way of dinner cleanup, but they normally cleared their cups and plates. Wynn hopped up to clear his cup, far more enthusiastic than she'd ever seen him. "Maybe while you're loading the dishwasher, Clemmie, Mr. Liam can meet Bo Peep."

"Yeah." Annie grabbed her cup. "She's the cutest lamb on the planet. Mr. Liam wants to see her and my box of rocks."

Did he? He'd been great with the kids so far, but he was not a family man. Clementine didn't want to put him out.

Before she could intervene, however, Liam stood up. "I'd love to see the rocks and meet Bo Peep."

It sure didn't look like he was fibbing to protect the kids' feelings. "Are you sure?"

"Who wouldn't want to see a treasure box and the cutest lamb on the planet?" With an almost flirtatious smile, he brushed past her to carry his plate to the counter by the sink. "I'm ready when you are, guys."

They started with the rocks, but it wasn't long before she heard the screen door open and shut, indicating they were heading to look at the lambs. It took her less than ten minutes to pack the leftovers in the fridge, load the dishwasher, wipe down the table and set out the paperwork they'd need to discuss festival matters. Once ready, Clementine strode out to the closest pasture, where Liam, the kids and both dogs were surrounded by lambs and their mamas. Bo Peep, however, snuggled secure in Wynn's arms.

"She grazes in the fields and eats grain, too," Wynn was saying in a formal-sounding voice, "but when she was a newborn, we fed her bottles. She grew fast, and now she's one of the biggest lambs in our flock. She's gonna be as good a ewe as her mom, Lady Bird."

Whoa. Wynn wasn't just showing off his favorite lamb. He was practicing for the pet show at the festival. While it wasn't a contest, she'd told him and Annie that the people walking through the event hall might ask questions about the pets, and the owners needed to be ready to answer them.

Her heart swelled, watching her nephew.

Annie stepped in front of Liam, commanding his attention. "Bo Peep is gonna be wearing a bow, okay? And she'll be all clean. No mud on her hooves."

"I can imagine it." Liam's lips twitched. "Great job, you two. You're definitely ready to show her off at the festival."

"Thanks for listening to me practice."

"I'm honored you'd practice on me. And you're right, Annie. Bo Peep is the cutest lamb on the entire planet."

Gently, Wynn lowered Bo Peep to the ground. "Clemmie says love is what makes a pet pretty, but we think Bo Peep is cute no matter what."

After a few more minutes with the animals, they returned to the house. She set the kids up with a cartoon movie and joined Liam at the dining table, where they surveyed the materials she'd laid out a few minutes ago, from vendors' applications to signed waivers and a chart.

They went over their tasks and split them up evenly, until all that remained was to assign small-business owners to specific tables for the vendor fair. Clementine showed him the empty chart. "I'm happy to take this on, since I'm accustomed to selling at venues like this. I do farmers' markets all the time."

"Sure. Tell me this, though. Is there a disadvantage to being placed in one area or another?" Liam tapped his pencil on the rectangles she'd drawn to represent tables placed in the vendor area.

"Not necessarily, although I know for a fact Maude Donalson won't want her table next to mine."

"Competition in the soap market? Or is there some sort of bad blood there?"

"Oh, no, she's a friend from church, but she's allergic to wool. Rash, watery eyes, can't stop sneezing. I have to be careful when she and I go to lunch once a month or so that I'm not all sheepy." She smiled. "I don't want her placed beside the knit-goods table, either, for the same reason. I'm not sure if the scented candle table would bother her, so maybe we should place her between the tinsmith and the homemade hair bows."

He held his hand up in a gesture of surrender. "Agreed. You're the best person to assign placement."

"That's it for now." Clementine stacked her papers. "Did you think of any questions about the festival?"

"Not the festival, but I'm wondering when I can clean out your gutters."

He was serious about that? "You don't have to clean my gutters."

"I know, but I want to and they need it. You and Rex have reasons to let someone else do it, all right? I just can't do it for a few days. Grandma and I are driving to Los Angeles tomorrow to visit Sara."

She whistled. That was a long drive. "Say hi to Sara for me and let me know if you need me to take back a festival task. I'd rather you visit with your family than call the radio station about Gretchen's interview or confirming recipe entrants. No worries on the gutters, either. You're supposed to be resting while you're here. Healing."

"I saw the doctor Wednesday, and she said I was doing well. I got rehab exercises to do and everything." He demonstrated by wiggling his fingers. "Speaking of healing, though, I have a present before I go. Well, not a present. But I hope it's helpful." He dug into his festival folder.

Clementine's heart thumped hard and fast. She had no idea what he was talking about, but he'd taken time to do something for her.

And despite her best intentions, she felt almost giddy. Eager to see what he'd done with her in mind.

Help me stop this, Lord. Would she ever be able to think of Liam without her heart doing somersaults in her chest?

Chapter Six

The sight of Liam's once-familiar handwriting on the cream-colored note card hit Clementine somewhere long forgotten within her heart. But the words he'd written hit her even harder. "You wrote out Bible verses for me?"

"I felt awful when you told me about your panic attacks. Still do. There's not a lot I can do, but I thought a list of verses might come in handy when you're feeling anxious. I'm new to the Bible, so I had to go online for help, but I found more verses on anxiety than I expected. Clearly, you're not the only person throughout history to have a hard time with worry." He shrugged. "Anyway, I'm sure you know about these Scriptures already, but I thought you might like to pull them out when you're having a panic attack. So you remember God cares about you."

He'd included verses from the Old and New Testaments about God's peace and compassion, including the first few verses of Psalm 23. *The Lord is my Shepherd*, which was fitting, considering her life was built around sheep.

What a gift, for Liam to make up this card for her.

"Benton and I meet on a semiregular basis since Brielle died." She didn't advertise the fact, but it was no secret. She wasn't ashamed to admit she'd needed prayer and counsel over the past few, difficult years. "He's a good pastor, reminding me God is patient and loving no matter how I feel. These verses say the same." She glanced up at him. "Thank you, Liam. I'll post this where I can see it every day."

"The soap shop?" he teased. "Milking stanchion?"

"If I tape it to my bathroom mirror, I'll see it first thing in the morning, so that's where I'll put it."

Of course, that meant she'd think of Liam first thing every day. And last thing before she went to bed. He was already on her mind more than she wanted him to be. Seeing him tonight—earlier, with a playful spark in his eyes while he interacted with the kids, and now, receiving the thoughtful gift of his writing out Scriptures for her—she was reminded yet again of the many reasons she'd cared for him so deeply all those years ago.

Liam Murphy was a special person, and there would always be a connection there. Thinking of him first thing in the morning might not help her get over him, but it was worth it to see that note card with the reminder of God's love for her. And a reminder to pray for Liam, wherever in the world his adventures would take him.

Liam watched Clementine finger the edges of the thick paper note card, pleased she appreciated the verses. Once he finished writing up her card, he'd made another for himself but on a different theme. Being a new creation in God. He'd changed a lot since he was hit on the head in that cavern last year, but there was still so much he had to learn. So much he wanted to be.

Including being more helpful to others.

He'd lived for a long time only concerned with his own needs and wants. Since coming to faith, he'd been more intentional about forging friendships with his fellow crew members while they were out on location. He'd brought that sense of intentionality with him to Widow's Peak Creek, realizing he had been given an opportunity to care for Grandma. He wouldn't be able to stay long, of course, but he'd do a better job of visiting her in the future.

He could also help Clementine while he was here, though he'd have to ask God what that might be, beyond cleaning her gutters and helping with her festival tasks. His heart still ached a pinch over her breaking up with him years ago, but that didn't mean he wanted to be with her anymore. He'd moved on.

Had he totally forgiven her, though? Maybe not, considering how he latched on to her dumping him when he needed her most. He still wanted the best for her, though. Wanted to help her through this tough time in her life. And all he could think to do right now to help make that happen was ensure her business succeeded.

He tapped the page with the rectangle diagram for the vendor fair. "The vendor fair is only happening on one day of the festival. That's just one day for you to sell soap, and I want you to focus on your sales, not your volunteering. If something comes up for the festival that needs attention, I'll handle it."

"That means a lot, Liam. I confess I'm praying for God to provide financially through the vendor fair. You know there's a lot of work to do with the fence I share with Fergus. Plus the roof repairs, and it all costs money." She rubbed the nape of her neck. "But God has His ways of working things out."

"I'm happy to fix the roof, like I said."

"I know, and I appreciate it, but I'm going to call a roofer. Not that you wouldn't do a good job, but a professional is licensed, insured, trained and has all the necessary equipment."

"No, I get it. They're the pros." He rapped his fingers on the tabletop. "I'll pray for your finances, if that's okay with you. And I'm serious about the Saturday of the festival. I know we have the recipe contest, but I can handle that while you work the vendor fair. I'm guessing you depend on events like this to not only gain sales but to advertise yourself, too."

"Thanks, but I've hired a teenager to come in and work the table while we do the recipe contest. You're right, though. Events like farmers' markets make up the bulk of my first-time customers. It's how people get to know my products. I have an online store, but my website doesn't get a lot of traffic. I need to update it, maybe. One more thing for the to-do list."

"Let me take a peek at it." Opening a search engine on his phone, Liam pecked out Honeysuckle Farm, California with his forefinger. Her site came right up, and he clicked on it.

"It's not fancy. You can tell I did it myself." Clementine's gaze was down, as if she was embarrassed.

She shouldn't be. "It's clean, neat, and the snapshots of the sheep are perfect. But if you really want to jazz it up, what about film footage? A minimovie on the home page showing the property, the sheep, the soap-making process. Whatever you want, but it would make for engaging content, especially if edited well."

"Sounds almost as out of reach for my budget as a trip to Mars."

He smiled at her joke, but he was serious. "I'm doing it for the festival website. Why not let me do it for you, too? I can streamline your product pages, also, if you want."

"You're saying you design websites?" She batted her eyes to make clear she was teasing.

He'd always liked it when she did that eye-batting thing. Her brown lashes were long and thick, and he always found them beguiling.

But he wouldn't go down that road again. Now or ever. "I did my website—it's part of the job to put myself out there—so I do have some experience. Anyway, I have a few cameras with me, including a drone. It wouldn't take long to get some footage."

She bit her lip. "You're helping me with the festival and the gutters. I can't ask you to do the website, too."

"I've got plenty of spare time."

"What spare time? The festival is in four weeks."

"And I'm not going to be able to return to work for five weeks. I'll be in town for a full week after the festival, and that's plenty of time to film things for your website."

"All right. If you're up to it. Footage of the farm would be fun to see."

"I think it'll look amazing. What about more text, too? You're such a good writer, or at least, you used to be, and I can't see how that would've changed any. There's a lot you could say on the site about the farm. Its history, stuff like that." He hoped he hadn't overstepped. "Just a thought."

"No, it's worth considering, although I have no idea

about the farm's history. I suppose there are ways to find out who held the original deed. Maybe the first owner arrived during the gold rush."

"Maybe there was once gold in Blue Creek." Wouldn't that have been something?

"If there was, or in Widow's Peak Creek itself, it was panned out a long time ago, but I wouldn't mind a little gold to pay for an electric fence. The only gold around here, however, are the mica flakes I added to a special batch of soap just for the festival. I ought to send a bar home with you for Marigold. I have a stash in the other room. Be right back."

Liam gathered his things, then joined the kids in the family room. Giggling at the cartoon, they lay on a thick gray rug, Martha dozing between them. At his approach, Martha opened her large brown eyes and rose, ambling over to him.

Stroking the dog's soft fur, he let himself get lost in the moment. Happy kids, content dog, full stomach, while the setting sun cast a rich golden glow through the west-facing windows. Was this what a home life could feel like? Warm, pleasant, peaceful?

For some people. Not for him.

"Here you go." Clementine bounded into the room carrying a paper-wrapped rectangle. "Rose Gold for your grandma. Tell her I'd love her feedback before I sell it at the festival. I'd offer you one, but I figure it might be a little flowery for your tastes."

The subtle scents of rose and peach enveloped him, as sweet as Clementine herself. Shaking off the thought, he accepted the gift. "Yeah, maybe, but she'll love it. Thanks."

Fifteen minutes later, Liam parked on the street in front of Grandma's house. He wasn't the least bit surprised to find her sitting on one of the wicker chairs on her front porch. Was she enjoying the mild evening with her crochet hook and a skein of yarn, or was she using it as an excuse to watch for him?

Definitely the latter. She perked up at his approach like a dog sensing a treat. "How was your evening, dear one?"

"Nice." He sat in the chair beside her, biting back a smile. His answer wouldn't satisfy her at all. "How was your evening? What exactly did you do, again? You were kind of vague about your plans."

"Nice?" Grandma's eyes narrowed as she ignored his question. "That's it?"

"Yes. Was yours nice, too?"

She harrumphed. "Are you going to make me pry everything out of you?"

He let his smile free. "Teasing you, Grandma." He filled her in on the menu and the festival tasks before digging the bar of soap out of his workbag. "Clementine asked you to test it and let her know your thoughts before she sells it at the festival."

"It's her way of giving me a gift without saying it, dear one." Marigold took a long sniff of the soap. "Oh, I like this one. Fruity but flowery."

Now it was time to turn the tables on her. "I keep forgetting to tell you, but I met your friend on Monday."

"Which friend? I have a few, you know."

"Rex Rigsby. He said you were the finest lady in the county, or something to that extent."

"That's hogwash." But she looked pleased by the compliment.

"You both said the word *thingamabob* in conversation."

"What are you implying?"

"I'm not implying anything. All I've done is make

observations that he admires you and you both say the word *thingamabob*."

"Lots of people say *thingamabob*. Clementine might even say it."

"I haven't heard her say *thingamabob*, and even if she did, I know what you're doing. Trying to change the subject off you and on to me and Clementine. You know things with us are not like *that*. Not like you and Rex."

He fully expected her to jump all over the mention of Rex Rigsby, but to his surprise, she patted his cheek, smoothing down his beard with her warm fingers. "Oh, my dear boy, when it comes to that woman over at Honeysuckle Farm? For you, it's always been like *that*. And it always will be."

He stood up with a jolt, leaving her hand floating in midair. This was not a discussion he could have with Grandma. "I'm ready for a hot shower and a cold ice pack on my shoulder, in that order. Can I get you anything before I go back to the tiny house?"

At the shake of her head, he bent and kissed her check. "G'night, then. Love you."

"Love you."

Love for his family was all the love he allowed himself to experience. Well, for God, too. Then there was love of others in a general sense. But caring about anyone else so deeply that the thought of living without them was unbearable, unimaginable?

Never. He'd loved Clementine once, but that was in the past. And that was where it would firmly stay.

Chapter Seven

Easter Sunday came bright and warm, full of joy and tradition.

One of those traditions was an invitation to brunch at Marigold's house after church. Marigold had invited Clementine and the kids—and a host of others—to her annual Christmas Eve and Easter celebrations over the past few years, but she hadn't felt able to handle large celebrations after Brielle and Brad died. Her grief over her sister had been too palpable.

Lately, though, things seemed to have shifted to a new phase. She still ached for her sister and brother-in-law. Still ached for the kids, growing up without their parents. But last Christmas, she'd felt ready to accept Marigold's invitation and join in the crowd, and it had been wonderful.

So she'd accepted the invitation to join in today, too, even though she still had a tiny sliver of apprehension about being around Liam. Well, not apprehension. More like awareness that she still reacted to him. However, she was further down the road of getting over him than she'd been a week ago, wasn't she? And she hadn't had a panic attack in days.

So now that brunch was finished and the guests were mingling and wandering around the house and outside, why shouldn't she celebrate those milestones with cake?

Alone, she made her way to the dining room where the desserts had been set up and sliced herself a piece of cake. A decadent confection of orange syrup-soaked sponge, frosted with orange marmalade and cream icing, it was undoubtedly as loaded with calories as it was with flavor.

Faith Santos peeked in, and Clementine held out her plate. "Ooh, Faith. You'll appreciate this. Marmalade cake. Don't you think Marigold should enter it into the Gold Star Favorites contest at the festival? It's orangey-gold and sooo good I'm about to fall on the floor. Come taste it."

To Clementine's surprise, Faith hardly glanced at her plate. "I can't handle another bite. I must have overeaten."

Not hard to do, given the abundance of choices that had been set out on Marigold's table for the brunch buffet. Each of the guests had brought a side dish to share, but Marigold had provided ham and dessert. The dishes had all been cleared after lunch, making way for cookie trays, brownie bites and the marmalade cake. Clementine was grateful for the loose-belted fit of her floral Easter dress. "I ate too much, too, but I couldn't say no to this cake."

Faith took a half step back. "Right now, I can't even stand the smell of food. No offense."

Uh-oh. This seemed like something more than a too-full tummy. "Want me to find Tom? Or Leah? She's a nurse."

"I'm sure all I need is a little fresh air. Thanks,

though." Faith's smile was apologetic as she hurried off, hand pressed against the fitted waistband of her peach Easter dress.

Poor Faith. She must be exhausted, considering she was a newlywed and new stepmom who ran her own business, had a large role in Gold Rush Days and had just pulled off the gargantuan task of opening the town museum. It wouldn't be a surprise if Faith succumbed to a virus. Maybe Clementine should follow her to lend assistance.

Before she could, Marigold entered the dining room with Liam, eyes sparking. "Clementine, dear, it seems great minds think alike when it comes to sweets."

"I can't say no to dessert." Smiling, Liam handed Marigold a plate.

Concerned as she was for Faith, Clementine decided to give her friend a few minutes alone before she followed her. Might as well finish her dessert and catch up with the two Murphys. She hadn't seen Liam in over a week, when he'd come for dinner. In a minute, she'd ask about their trip to Los Angeles to see Sara, but first, she had a job to do as coordinator of the Gold Star Favorites contest.

"Marigold, you've got to enter this into the Gold Star Favorites contest."

Marigold's white eyebrows pulled into a skeptical line. "It's just a cake, dear."

"There is nothing *just* about this cake." When she savored the next bite, Clementine couldn't hold back a *mmm* noise.

She wished she'd kept quiet when she met Liam's gaze. Judging by that sly smile pulling at his cheeks, he was either in agreement about the fabulous nature of his grandma's cake or about to tease her. Royally.

"That good, huh?" He reached past her, the crisp sleeve of his pale blue dress shirt brushing her arm. He'd shed his blazer after church, and it was difficult not to stare at the well-defined muscles of his shoulders as he took a piece of cake.

Clementine forced her gaze to stay on the dessert, where it belonged. "Haven't you eaten this cake before?"

"Nope."

"New recipe," Marigold said. "Pardon me, but I hear someone calling my name." Waving her fingers, she exited the dining room with a grin.

Did the grin have anything to do with leaving Liam and Clementine alone in the dining room? Not that they were really alone. The house was full of people. Aside from Clementine and the kids, Faith and Tom Santos and his twins, and Liam, of course, she'd opened her home to numerous friends. Some had kids, like her lawyer friend Joel Morgan, here with his little girl, Maisie. Others were the grandparent-type, like Marigold's widowed friends, Maude, Eileen, Trudie and Rowena.

The neighbors were here, too. Kellan and Paige Lambert had come with their six-month-old daughter, Poppy. Bald and chubby, Poppy's cooing gurgles made Clementine ache to hold her. Benton got that fun assignment, however, and she could see him through the dining room window, cuddling the baby on the back porch to watch the older children like Wynn and Annie play with bubbles. Benton's new fiancée, Leah, came into view and handed him a burp cloth.

For such a crowded house, however, no one else was in the dining room but her and Liam, and Clementine was keenly aware of Liam's proximity. His cedarwood scent. His height and breadth. The richness of his deep brown eyes, sparking with laughter as he forked a bite of cake.

He made a show of savoring the morsel, tilting his head like he was thinking hard.

Clementine folded her arms. "Isn't it good?"

"No, it's not *good*." He set down the plate. "It's… I can't even think of a word. Except maybe…*mmm*."

He was about to find out that she could dish out the teasing as well as take it. "Are you trying to imitate me? Because you did a terrible job."

"I sounded exactly like you." Unoffended, he popped another bite into his mouth.

"You're incorrigible."

"You're fun to tease."

Oh, my, but she didn't want to enjoy sparring with him like this. She'd better change the subject. Thankfully, a rush of movement outside the dining room window gave her a ready topic. "I think the kids have been told dessert's available, because here they come."

"Glad I got my cake when I did," Liam joked.

Sure enough, the children rushed into the dining room. Nearly all of them reached for the iced cookies cut into familiar Easter shapes like crosses, eggs and bunnies. Pink bunny cookie in hand, Annie pointed at Liam's plate. "What's that?"

"Mrs. Murphy's marmalade cake."

Annie's eyes grew round. "Ma-ma-lade starts with *M*. Can I put the cake in my *M* bag, Clemmie?"

Clementine smiled at a clueless-looking Liam. "Preschool homework. Annie needs to find five things that begin with *M* to fit in a lunch sack for show-and-tell tomorrow. Annie, I don't think the cake would last well, but we have marmalade at home. You can help me put a spoonful into a plastic tub to show off instead."

Liam forked another bite. "What other *M* items do you have so far, Annie?"

"Play money and Wynn's mako shark toy." Annie's nose wrinkled. "Too bad it's not *R* week, because I have a red ball and ruby ring and my red rock collection."

"Let's see if we can figure out a few more *M* things." Liam scratched his chin. "What are some toys that start with *M*?"

Tom appeared in the dining room doorway, signaling to his twins. "Time to go, guys."

While the kids said their farewells, Clementine sidled alongside Tom. "I was about to come looking for Faith. How is she?"

"She'll be okay, but she needs to put her feet up."

"I'll pray for her." She bid the Santos kids goodbye and then met Liam's curious gaze. "Faith doesn't feel well. She seemed fine a few days ago. The kids played while she, Gretchen and I did some work for the festival." They'd crafted rustic-looking wood signs directing visitors to the festival's different areas, finalized maps for the guests and talked decorations. "I'm sure she's tired. She's been working overtime on organizing the historical interpreters. There's only three weeks to go and there's still so much to be done."

"We'll be ready. Sounds like your spring break wasn't all that restful. Did you sleep in at all?"

"The sheep don't care for me sleeping in late, but the kids and I had some fun. We dyed Easter eggs, played board games, ordered pizza." She scooped up her last bite of cake. "How was your trip? How are Sara and her husband?"

"Dane was busy with work and we hardly saw him, unfortunately." The loud vibration of a cell phone intruded halfway through his sentence, and he reached into his pocket to pull out the device. "That's Sara now. Just a sec, and I'll ask if I can call her back later."

"Go ahead and chat with her. I wanted to see if any of the ladies in the other room need dessert." Some of the older women used walkers and might prefer dessert brought to them rather than going to the dining room to get it.

Besides, if she stayed here, she'd be tempted to eat another piece of that amazing cake.

Liam took the phone out to the front porch and sat in one of Grandma's squeaky wicker rockers. "Happy Easter, sis."

"Hey." Sara didn't return his greeting acknowledging the holiday. "You left a book behind." She read off the title. "Want me to mail it up to you?"

No pleasantries, no chitchat? Was she in a hurry or something? "No, thanks. I'll pick it up next time I'm down. I do still technically live in the casita, right? You're getting my rent payments?" he joked.

"Of course. You always have a home with me, Liam. You know that."

Warning bells went off in his head, loud and shrill as a fire alarm. "What's going on, Sara? Are you okay?"

"I hear people in the background. Are you out somewhere?"

"Grandma's got a full house for postchurch brunch. Easter Sunday—"

"Sorry, I forgot she did that. We can talk later."

"No worries. We've eaten, everyone's chatting and I'm thinking you called about more than that book."

Other than a long sigh, she was quiet for several seconds. "I don't know who else to talk to. It's about Dane."

Liam sat up straighter. He'd known his sister's marriage had hit a rough patch, which was why he'd decided to recuperate in Widow's Peak Creek with Grandma, rather than in the casita. But last week when he and Grandma visited at Sara's invitation, everything seemed okay between Sara and Dane. Except for Dane's hectic work schedule, of course. "Is that why he was gone so much?"

"Bingo." She sniffled.

"I'm sorry, sis. I want to help if I can."

"No one can help. Oh, Liam, Dane wants a baby. Babies."

Now he understood why Sara said only he could understand her. "I thought you talked about it before you got married, and he was okay with you not wanting any."

"He's had a change of heart. I can't blame him for wanting kids, but no matter how much I might want a baby, I can't be a mom, not with the role model we had. At some point or another, I'd yell at them the way Mom yelled at us. I wouldn't want to, I would try hard not to, but I know I'd make mistakes that I can't take back. I mean, we were made to feel at fault for existing. What if I did that to my kid? I don't want to damage a child."

"I know what you mean." How often had he and Sara heard that if they hadn't been born, Mom's life would have been so much easier? Better? Dad hadn't verbalized any of it, but he'd preferred hiding away in his art studio. "You and I would try so hard not to be like Mom and Dad, but it's all we know. I'd be so scared one of Mom's favorite phrases would slip out."

I had to give that up when you were born...

If I hadn't had kids...

Sara's sigh was long and loud. "Dane doesn't understand."

"Neither does Grandma. They mean well, though."

"You were smart to stay single. I thought marriage would be easier if Dane and I didn't have kids, but I was wrong. Clearly, our communication skills aren't that hot." Her breath hitched, like she'd been crying. "I don't know what's going to happen."

"I don't, either, but I'll be praying for you and Dane to figure this out." Hopefully together, although he had no clue how the pair of them could meet in the middle over something like this. He well remembered six years ago when Sara told him she wanted to marry Dane, and even though she was scared because their parents' relationship hadn't been healthy, she'd been optimistic she could do better than they had.

Liam had hoped for the best for them. Still did. But now that he knew God, Liam recognized that God could accomplish their full restoration. He'd pray for them, not just for their marriage, but for them to encounter God.

Sara was quiet for a moment. "I'm not sure God will listen, but I suppose it couldn't hurt."

"God hasn't answered all my prayers the way I want Him to, but that doesn't mean He never listened." There was comfort in that. Peace.

Well, some peace. He wasn't even sure what he was praying for when it came to Clementine, though. For so long he'd wanted to just forget her. Now he realized he might not have completely forgiven her for wounding him way back when. Getting to know her anew was helping with that, but he should pray for her more. Pray for closure. For her happiness. After all, that's what he really wanted for her, wasn't it? For her success, safety and happiness?

Liam sat on the porch for a few minutes after the end of his conversation with his sister, praying and mulling, until Joel Morgan and his little girl, Maisie, stepped out onto the porch, carrying an empty wood salad bowl.

"Hey," Joel said. "I wondered where you went. See you at Bible study Wednesday?"

"I'll be there." Before he finished his short sentence, Wynn, Annie and Clementine came out to the porch. Grandma brought up the rear. "There you are, Liam."

"Is everything all right?" Clementine glanced at the phone still in his hand.

"I forgot a book at Sara's. Hey, kids, have great days at school tomorrow. Have fun finding more *M* items for your bag, Annie."

"I found them already. One is Maisie."

"How do you plan to fit an elementary school student into a paper bag?"

Annie giggled, just as he'd hoped she would. "Not her body. Her picture. Mr. Joel had one in his wallet an' he said I could keep it because he has lots. Maisie's my friend forever." Annie weaved her chubby fingers through Maisie's and squeezed three times. "And Wynn remembered another *M* at home. *Mustache*."

Liam bit back a laugh. "A mustache?"

"There are a few in the dress-up bin." Clementine shifted the empty white casserole from one hand to another. "They glue on."

"That'll be some *M* bag." Liam shoved his phone into his pants pocket. "Maybe I can see the mustache later this week. I was thinking I could come clean out your gutters. The weather forecast is partly cloudy and cool, so this is a good time to do it."

"You're telling me," Joel said. "That's why I'm starting on Clementine's barn tomorrow. Roofing in the blazing sun is awful."

Wait, what? "*You're* fixing the barn roof?"

Clementine had said she wanted someone licensed. Someone who was trained. Joel was no professional roofer. Wasn't he a lawyer?

A large black pit of jealousy stretched open in Liam's gut, gnawing at him with sharp teeth. So that's how it was. Clementine didn't want a roofer after all. It was just that she preferred Joel—big as an ox, square-jawed, decent-looking Joel—to do it. Not Liam.

Completely oblivious to the storm raging inside of Liam, Joel rubbed the back of his neck. "Yeah. My case-load is light for the next few weeks, so I've got time to put on my hard hat. I'm a licensed contractor, and every so often, I take on a project. Good to keep busy."

"Huh." It was all Liam could think to say. Joel being a contractor didn't really make him feel any better.

"I already did an inspection, and it'll only take me a day. So if you want to start on the gutters later in the week, that's great. We won't be overlapping."

Clementine's bright-eyed gaze locked on to Liam's. "That works for me, Liam. We can talk festival stuff, too. But for now, I need to get these two kiddos home. Thanks for having us, Marigold."

As she hugged Grandma, Joel shook Liam's hand. "Happy Easter, brother."

"And to you." Brother.

Liam liked the sentiment of being brothers in Christ

with other guys, but right now, much as he liked Joel…? The jealous beast in his belly was still grumbling. It didn't help when he watched Joel, Clementine and the three kids walk together out to their cars, parked on the street.

Grandma nudged his ribs with her elbow. "You're scowling at Joel. What'd he do?"

"Nothing. And I'm not scowling."

She snorted. "There's nothing going on with Joel and Clementine, in case you're wondering."

He couldn't lie, but he didn't want to confirm her suspicion, either. "I was just thinking they have a lot in common. Raising kids on their own." Did they have anything else in common, too? Like romantic feelings? "They're clearly close, since he's helping her with her roof."

"Don't get in a dither because she asked him and not you. It makes perfect sense to me why she did that."

"I get it. He's licensed."

Her laugh came out like a spurt. "The license thingamabob is nice, yes, but this isn't about which of you wields a hammer better. Clementine, in case you haven't noticed, is more anxious than she used to be. It's one thing to be fearful about a man falling off your roof when you don't have feelings for him beyond friendship. But when it's a man you love?"

"Clementine hasn't loved me in sixteen years. If ever."

Grandma sighed, like he was the world's biggest idiot.

She was wrong. Sweet, but wrong. Clementine didn't have feelings for him, and he didn't have any for her.

But hours later, he was still thinking about Joel Morgan fixing her roof, and he still didn't like it one bit.

Chapter Eight

Later that week, Clementine exited the soap shed, carrying a paperboard box on her hip. Since she'd entered her workshop a half hour ago, Liam had moved the ladder to the north side of the house. His back was to her as he balanced near the top of the ladder, scooping out the gutter with a gloved hand.

She paused, blocking the morning sun from her eyes with her hand, to watch him work. He wore jeans, boots, and instead of a sling, a brace of some sort weaved around both his shoulders and wrapped around his faded black T-shirt. His dark hair swooshed in the back in such a way that, were she young again, she'd want to touch and see if a curl locked around her finger.

He was as handsome as when he was seventeen but also as hungry for adventure as ever. It wasn't just his job. It was him, always eager to see and do new things despite the risks involved. He gave his all, plus a little extra, whatever he was doing. Even now. His arms were long and strong, yes, but did he have to stretch out so far to scoop decaying leaves and debris from the gutters? He was an inch from losing his balance, and all thoughts of his swooshy hair vanished when he reached farther out, and her stomach tightened into a hard ball of nerves.

Lord, please don't let him fall. Please.

She didn't feel this anxious when Joel was on the roof the other day. Maybe because he was harnessed in. Or maybe because she was distracted by the kids while Joel worked, since he'd brought Maisie along.

But Liam wasn't even up on the roof right now. What he was doing was far less precarious than what Joel had done. She started to scold herself over her lack of trust in God—her lack of faith—when Liam glanced over his shoulder at her.

"What's up?"

My anxiety level.

Clementine paused at the foot of the ladder amid a pile of decaying leaves that had come out of the gutter but missed the nearby refuse bin. "I packed a box of thank-you gifts for the festival volunteers. There are so many people chipping in who aren't on the main committee, like Leah Dean and her friend Irene, who are working the first aid station. They're not much, though."

"They sound big to me, Clementine. Truly thoughtful." Liam descended the ladder.

"Only if you appreciate sheep-milk soap." She gave a self-deprecating chuckle.

"Well, I do. Especially the cedar one." He peered into the box, close enough that she caught a whiff of his masculine scent. "Soaps and— What are those?"

"Wool scrubbies. For doing dishes." Her head started to spin at his nearness, so she stepped away and lowered the box onto the porch steps. He'd set out her rake, propping it against the banister, and she gathered it to clean up the mess that had missed the refuse bin. "Thanks again for doing this. You were right about how clogged the gutters were."

"I didn't intend for you to clean up, though."

"How did you intend to rake with one arm?"

"I'd have figured something out. So, how did the roof repair go?" He shifted the bin so she could more easily rake leaves into it.

"Great. I'm glad Joel had the time to do it."

"The guy's a contractor and a lawyer. Doesn't seem like there's much he can't do."

"Seriously." He was a much more confident single parent than Clementine, but the guy seemed fearless. Like Liam. "Anyway, it's a relief that it's done. Same with the festival chores. I completed my task list and asked Faith if I could help her out. She sounded worlds better on the phone, though, and said she's all done with stuff."

"I've done everything on my checklist, too. How about your vendor task list?" He moved the ladder and ascended again. "Are you ready to sell soap?"

"Sure am." There was one last batch curing that she could package next week, and she'd confirmed the teenager she'd hired would be at the soap table while she was busy with the recipe contest and the kids' pet event. "You've lightened my load a lot."

"I have lots of time on my hands. I helped Gretchen earlier this week with all the items we'd talked about. Got her booked on morning radio, and we worked on footage for the social media pages. I filmed her panning for gold—not really, but pretending to—things like that, for a short video for the website. She'll pop it online tonight. While we were at it, we decided I'd film during the festival so that's available for promotion next year. Assuming there's a festival next year, but it's sure to be a hit."

"I can't wait to see the video." She tried to focus on how great his work would be rather than the fact that he'd spent so much time with Gretchen over the past few days. They were coworkers on the festival team.

But even if they wanted to date, it was none of Clementine's business. Any residual feelings she still had for him had to go, go, go.

She raked with more vigor than was necessary, and all was quiet except for the bleats of sheep, the breeze sliding through the cottonwood leaves and the sounds of their work, splats of emptying gutters and the *scritch* of the rake.

Until the rake caught on something that felt wrong. She nudged her toe into the slimy, decaying leaves and found a damp, reddish-brown rock. "Was this up in the gutter?"

"Beats me, but if it's red, maybe Annie would like it for her collection."

Oh yeah—Annie had shown Liam her treasure box of rocks when he was here for dinner. "I'll set it aside for her, but so far all of them have come from the creek. Kind of surprising how many rust-red ones there are. She says she's going to make a brick house out of them someday and live in it."

His soft laugh carried down to her. "She's a funny kid. Wynn's a great kid, too, Clementine. They're both amazing but have totally different personalities."

"He's a homebody like me, but she's fearless. If the ladder's still here when she gets home from school, she'll want to climb it." She might have said more, but Dolley's bark put a stop to any chitchat.

Liam turned with her to search out the Great Pyrenees. Dolley stood apart from the sheep, near the southern fence by the main road, her posture alert. "What's wrong?"

"I don't know. That's not her warning bark, but something's bugging her." Clementine jogged to the fence and let herself through the gate, Liam at her heels. A quick count of the sheep set her skin prickling, a sign of an impending panic attack. "Lady Bird's missing. So are her lambs."

"They can't have gone far. That's what the fence is for."

In theory, yes, but the fact still stood that Lady Bird and her three babies had vanished. Two of them were scheduled to be sold to a breeder, but Bo Peep had been chosen to be a permanent resident of Honeysuckle Farm. "Bo Peep is one of Lady Bird's lambs. You know how much she means to Wynn and Annie."

"We'll find them all." Liam's strong voice was comforting as they hurried toward the far fence. "There's another fence between this field and the street, right?"

"Yes, to protect the garden and the blackberry bushes." She understood Liam's point: the sheep would have had to wander through the garden area to get to the street, so two separate fences protected them from traffic.

Unless thieves had taken them—

Don't think like that. It didn't make sense anyway. How would a thief know to take Lady Bird and her lambs, and only their family unit? Clementine scanned for a gap in the fence.

"Argh, there it is."

The rip started at the ground and went high enough for a sheep to fit through. And sure enough, the bleat of a frustrated sheep from the garden was all the assurance she needed that Lady Bird was inside. She led Liam around to the gate, and from this vantage, they could see the wooly bodies of Lady Bird, Bo Peep and one of the male lambs, which the children had dubbed Boy Blue, caught in the thick of the brambles. The other male, which Wynn and Annie had named Baa Baa, was content to munch a tufted weed at his mother's hind feet.

Relieved as she was to find them, a frustrated sigh escaped her throat.

"What? Are the berry bushes toxic to them?"

"No, that's not it. Just that Fergus is right. How do I keep missing these tears in my fences?"

"I doubt you missed anything, Clementine. It's got to be a new tear, because you and Rex check weekly, right?"

"Right." Once through the gate, Clementine squatted to assess the situation, then gave Lady Bird's back a gentle pat. "It's all right, love. We'll get you out in no time." Brambles scratched her arms, and oh boy, the bees were thick here, too. Trying to ignore their buzzing, Clementine prayed she wouldn't get stung. Gently, gently, she maneuvered Lady Bird's head from the bush. Lady Bird tolerated it patiently, not moving except for her occasionally shifting feet.

Thank you, Lord, that she's not fighting me.

Liam rubbed the now-free Lady Bird on the head. "Looks like LB fared better than you, Clementine. Those are some mean scratches."

"Eh." She hardly noticed.

"I'll get the next one. I'm wearing gloves. Well, a glove." Liam gestured at his healing left arm and then reached into the bush.

"Gloves only protect your hands. Your arm will get scratched up—"

"It's okay." He scooped Boy Blue in his right arm. "That wasn't too hard, was it, buddy? Now for your sister."

Bo Peep was in too far to get with one hand, though, so he gave Clementine his glove. The lamb resisted, fighting in fear, her high-pitched bleats breaking Clementine's heart and making Lady Bird fretful. Clementine needed to get the lamb out, fast. "Relax, little one. I've got you. Trust me."

At last, she disentangled Bo Peep from the bush and snuggled her to her chest. "The kids are going to fuss over you tonight, aren't they?"

The kids. She'd lost all track of time. Annie would be out of school soon. Clementine checked her watch. It was later than she thought. "I've got to pick up Annie. I'm so sorry to leave you like this, Liam. Thanks for your help with the gutters. How can I repay you?"

"Just go get Annie. I'll move these guys back where they belong."

She wanted to say more, do more to express her appreciation for his help and presence, but she couldn't leave Annie waiting. She rushed inside the house, grabbed her purse and left him in the berry patch. Hopefully, he knew how to get the sheep back to the field.

Thankfully, every traffic signal between Honeysuckle Farm and Little Lambs Preschool was green, so Clementine was able to make it in record time. Paige Lambert, one of the aides and a dear friend, was at the desk with the sign-out sheets. Since Paige had a young baby, she worked part-time, and Clementine knew it was time for the brunette to go home for the day. She hurriedly scribbled her name on Annie's class list. "Sorry I'm late, Paige. I hope I didn't keep you."

"Not at all. Is everything okay? Some parents are always running behind, but not you."

"One of the ewes and her lambs got caught in a berry bush."

"I'd hoped you were doing something more fun, like having a lunch date with Liam."

Clementine dropped the pencil. Then picked it up off the floor and smacked it too hard on the counter. "What? No. I mean, he's at my house to clean out my gutters, but he's also helping me with the festival—"

"The festival committee. Yeah." Paige's grin said she thought more was going on than Clementine and Liam working on a recipe contest and gutters.

Thankfully, Annie burst through the door to the classes and rushed into her arms. Perfect timing.

Annie patted her stomach. "I'm hungry."

"Hello to you, too." She kissed Annie's head, then waved to Paige. "See you later."

"Tell Liam hi for me."

As if Paige weren't his next-door neighbor. She'd see him first, because he'd be long gone from Honeysuckle Farm by the time Clementine and Annie got back.

Except Liam's car was still there. He was no longer in the garden but in the field with the sheep. Hopefully, it hadn't taken him this long to get the sheep back here.

Annie let herself into the field gate and rushed to him. "What are you doing, Mr. Liam?"

"Hoping I'm not overstepping." He shifted back, allowing Clementine to see that he'd secured the gap in the fence with zip ties and portable plastic fencing, like she'd done when Eleanor got out last time. "I took these from the barn. It might not be the best long-term option, but I didn't want any sheep to visit the berry patch again."

Annie had lost interest already, crouched on the ground to fuss over the lambs, but Clementine couldn't tear her gaze from his patchwork. "It's perfect. Really. Thank you, but I don't know how you did it without two hands."

"I do have two hands." He wiggled the fingers of his left hand. "I just can't use my shoulder yet. The only thing?" He stepped closer, his face serious. Whatever he had to say, he didn't want Annie to overhear it. "The hole in the fence? It was clean. Neat. It's deliberate, Clementine. Someone is sabotaging your fences."

Liam hated to share his suspicions with Clementine, but she needed to know if someone was sabotaging her farm. He expected confusion, or maybe outrage, but instead she shook her head.

"Why would anyone want to do that?" She squatted, peering at the wire edges he'd pulled together with plastic zip ties. "It's so low to the ground. No human could get in through that size of a hole, all the way down there. Why not use the gate? Why go in there at all? There aren't even berries yet. It's too early."

Liam agreed it was weird. A weird-sized hole in a weird place. But there was no denying the wire looked like it had been cut with a tool. "I don't know, Clementine, but it seems suspicious."

"I don't know how it happened, but it confirms I need a new fence." Standing, she brushed bits of damp grass off her jeans.

"I'm sorry." Not his fault, but he hated the amount of responsibility and stress she bore.

"It's patched up, though, thanks to you. You've been a huge help to me, Liam. Not just with this but everything."

Had he? He hoped so, but right now all he felt was… confused. Like he wanted to learn how to fix fences so she and her beloved animals would be protected. To stay here and keep watch for a friend in need.

Gretchen is a friend, too, but you didn't offer to clean out her gutters.

Enough of that type of thinking. Liam told Clementine and Annie goodbye and returned to the tiny house, determined to just be grateful he and Clementine seemed to be friends again. Maybe by the time the festival was over, they'd be the kind of friends who kept in touch.

God willing, it would be nice to be friends like that.

It certainly felt like a friend-thing to do when she texted him later that evening while he was enjoying a dish of ice cream and the sports channel on television.

Gretchen posted your footage online. Looks great! Love the combination of action + nature shots. You made our little neck of the woods look spectacular.

Praise was always nice, but when it came from Clementine, it filled him with a true sense of accomplishment. He pecked out a reply of thanks.

It's easy to make the creek look good.

Within two minutes, she responded. He set down his bowl of rocky road ice cream to read her reply.

Not just the creek. You also shot the bridge and the Main Street shops. So smart to showcase places tourists can visit after the festival.

It was silent a moment except for three dots, indicating she was still typing.

You even included the Daffodil Spot.

How could he not? It was a true tourist draw. A Dutch immigrant had planted hundreds of bulbs on their ranch during the gold rush era to remind the family of their homeland. Now, generations later, the land still belonged to the same family, and they planted new bulbs each autumn for visitors to enjoy in the spring.

It had significance to him and Clementine, too. Or at least, to him. They'd picnicked there on their first real date. He'd been fifteen years old, so nervous he could hardly swallow his peanut butter sandwich. Clementine had been prettier than the sea of yellow and white flowers around them.

That was a long time ago but had felt like yesterday when he went over there to capture the daffodils on film.

Did she remember that day, too? Or had she formed other happy memories of the Daffodil Spot in the sixteen years that had passed?

Have you been over to see them?

Her reply was instant. She hadn't, so he suggested she do so before the daffodils faded. It was almost May, so time was short for the blooms. He almost offered to go with her and the kids, but he chickened out. They might be friends again, but he didn't want to push it.

But they kept on texting, and his ice cream had melted into a thin soup by the time he picked up his bowl again.

Over the next week, Liam's days fell into a pleasant rhythm. Time with Grandma and assisting her around the house interspersed with weekday lunches with some of the guys from men's Bible study. Even Joel, and Liam was relieved when the topic of dating came up and the burly lawyer said he was focusing on Maisie for the foreseeable future.

Not that Liam had a claim to Clementine. Nevertheless, he spent almost every afternoon and evening with her and the kids, shopping for festival supplies, or squeezing last-minute applicants into the vendors' fair space. They'd secured three judges for the Gold Star Favorites contest, including the principals of the elementary and secondary schools and Mayor Judy Hughes.

She didn't have any other chores for him, but he was happy to join her walking the perimeter fence to look for weaknesses. Her grumpy neighbor, Fergus, watched them, so Liam waved, but Fergus didn't wave back.

Thankfully, Grandma didn't make any more comments about his time with Clementine. Likewise, he didn't overthink their time together. He'd spent the last several years living in the moment, and that's what he did now. Enjoying where he was, right here and now.

One early evening, a week before the festival, the kids played on the family room floor while Liam and Clementine worked at the dining table, charts and papers and her laptop computer between them. Clementine stretched her arms. "Dinner's in the Crock-Pot. Nothing fancy, just beef-and-barley soup, toast and salad, but would you like to stay? Or do you have plans?"

The soup's rich aroma made his stomach growl. "I'd love to. Smells delicious. Grandma's busy with some mysterious meeting tonight, so I was just going to make a sandwich." He reached for his elbow. His collarbone was aching again, and sometimes, he caught himself fidgeting with his arm without thinking.

"Just a sec." Clementine popped into the kitchen and opened the freezer. She returned with a package of peas. "I don't have an ice pack, but maybe this will help."

She'd noticed his discomfort? "I don't want to ruin your vegetables."

"I'll use them to make a cold pea salad for tomorrow. Go on, use it."

He draped the package of peas over his shoulder, liking how it conformed to the contours of his neck and collarbone. "Perfect. Thanks."

Resuming her seat at the dining table, she slid a finger across the touchpad . "Before I close up the laptop, I'll get on social media to promote the festival page again. Since your footage was posted, Gretchen said the site's gotten a lot more traffic."

At the sound of the music Gretchen had picked to accompany the video, Wynn left his toys to stand at Clementine's shoulder. "That's a nice movie."

"Liam filmed that. Didn't he do a great job?"

"I wanna see." Annie clambered into Clementine's lap.

The footage was ingrained in Liam's memory. The rushing creek flowing in its V-shaped bend around the boulder in Hughes Park. Gretchen's hands going through the motions of panning for gold. The daffodils swaying in the breeze. Faith in an old-fashioned green dress, demonstrating how to use a spinning wheel. The display of books on town history at Kellan's bookstore,

Open Book, and other points of interest from the shops on historic Main Street. Hughes House, the beautiful old home that now served as the Widow's Peak Creek Museum. He'd even filmed some of the exhibits to showcase the area's history.

"How many movies have you made, Mr. Liam?" Wynn's eyes were bright.

"A few." It was an understatement, but he'd lost count.

"I wanna watch another one." Annie leaned against Clementine's chest.

Clementine's questioning gaze met Liam's. What was she asking? If he minded? Of course he didn't, and he'd never filmed anything that wasn't family-friendly. He'd never thought of his projects in those terms, but he'd gotten to know Wynn and Annie enough to have an idea what they might like. "There's one on animal camouflage, with zebras and tigers and geckos."

Wynn pumped his fist. "Tigers."

"Zebras." Annie mimicked his fist pump.

Within two minutes, they were squished on the couch together while the streaming service loaded.

How long had it been since he sat on a couch with friends to do something—watch a show, play a game, relax? Even when he was between work projects, staying at the casita behind Sara and Dane's place, he kept himself too busy to think.

Too busy to feel. Right now, though, he was feeling all sorts of things, none of them easy to grapple with. Peace. A newfound desire to connect with people, like he'd felt that first time he'd gone to the men's Bible study group.

Times like this with his own family had been few

and far between, but he wasn't surprised Clementine's house was one of tranquility. Her parents had been wonderful. So had Brielle. Caring, interested, giving. Just the sort of family he'd wanted for himself when he expected to share his future with Clementine.

Her gaze drew his like a tether. With Annie snuggled against her, she watched him instead of the screen, her damp eyes reflecting light and an emotion he couldn't figure out.

Whatever it was, it was serious. His heart almost jumped out of his chest. What was Clementine thinking?

Chapter Nine

Clementine couldn't speak around the lump in her throat, looking at Liam.

He'd done wonderful work. Beautiful work. And oh, she was so glad she'd set him free to do it. To be whom God made him to be.

The kitchen timer's buzz jolted her. "That's the soup. Go wash up for dinner, kids."

"Aww. I like the baby zebra," Annie grumbled but obeyed anyway, following her brother to their bathroom.

After pausing the show, Liam joined Clementine in the kitchen. He set the frozen peas on the counter while she wiped her clean hands on the black-striped dish towel hanging off the oven door. "Is everything okay? It seemed like…well, like something was going on back there."

She popped bread into the toaster. "Your work."

"Did it give you a panic attack? That tiger shot looked like I was right up next to it, but it wasn't even close. Long-range lenses. Totally safe. And filmed five years ago. Not a scratch on me." He held up his right arm.

"I beg to differ. You're totally scratched up from the berry bushes," she teased. "And no, I didn't panic."

Panic was the furthest thing from her mind right now. She felt the opposite, in fact. Remembering those well-muscled arms pulling her close. Those moments before he used to kiss her, when the air felt electrified, as if lightning were about to strike.

She had to tear her gaze away. Those were memories she must not indulge in, now or ever. Getting bowls out of the cupboard, she forced her thoughts back to what she'd been mulling in the family room. The matter at hand. *Divergent paths, remember?*

"You're so talented, Liam. I knew it already, of course, but seeing this? It's obvious your job suits you in every way."

His relieved smile revealed the top of a dimple in his left cheek, right above the edge of his beard. "It's not work to me. It's pure privilege."

It was a strong reminder that she and Liam may have had a moment in time, but their paths would have diverged sooner or later. He was where he belonged, traveling the globe, capturing the wonders of God's creation on film for others' education and benefit.

And she was where she belonged, too, here at home, doing her best to give Wynn and Annie the stable, secure life they deserved.

She'd been right to break up with him sixteen years ago. If only the old wound didn't still sting. Even so, she must be grateful for the insights God was giving her now. It was confirmation that they were both where they were supposed to be. And that they could still be part of one another's lives as friends.

She held on to that mindset over the rest of the evening as well as the following days. Liam was at the house most evenings, keeping the kids company while she milked the ewes, talking about updates to her website, and playing games. Being with Liam had become so natural again, they even sat together in church on Sunday, the first of May. She was pretty sure both of them were praying about the festival, which was now only five days away.

Thursday, the day before the festival opened, they spent hours transforming the fairgrounds with the other volunteers. With his arm still in a sling, Liam couldn't help set up tables, but he hauled signs and unpacked box after box, putting in as much, or more, effort than the others. Clementine appreciated his dedication.

She put in some hard work, too, and only left to get the kids from their various schools. She had to bring them back with her, but the Santos twins were here now, too, and between her, Liam, Tom and Faith, the kids were always under supervision.

By the late afternoon, there wasn't much left to do. Liam climbed on a ladder to string lights over the dining area, a picnic-table-filled rectangle set up beside a field where the food trucks would be parked by this time tomorrow. The thought of the food trucks' offerings made Clementine's mouth water. And if she were getting hungry, the kids would soon be ravenous. They were out of her sight right now, playing on the other side of a hedge, but they'd been with Tom. Any minute now, she expected them to come running, complaining of empty bellies. "Good thing we're almost done," she called up to Liam as she handed him another length of string lights. "It's almost dinnertime."

"Want to go to DeLuca's for pizza? Tom told me everyone's welcome to head over with the group tonight."

She'd planned to invite Liam to join her and the

kids for hamburgers, but a group thing involving all the volunteers sounded appropriate, considering they'd all worked so hard together. Besides, much as she'd enjoyed time alone with Liam and the kids the past few weeks, it wouldn't be a bad idea to widen her social circle back up. At the end of next week, he'd be gone.

She blinked. A week? That was all the time he had left in Widow's Peak Creek?

"Earth to Clem," he joked.

"Sorry. Yeah, we'd love pizza." She hadn't realized her hands had gone still.

"Are you concerned about getting back to the farm for milking?"

"Rex is covering for me tonight."

"So you get a break from chores, then."

"And a break from Fergus."

"He's still bugging you?"

Every opportunity he got. "He's persistent, I'll give him that. But I'm not selling to him." She would've vented about her neighbor more, but the kids running around the corner put a stop to that line of conversation. Their faces revealed twin expressions of utter seriousness. That usually meant they had something to ask her. "Yes, my loves?"

"Clemmie, the stuff for the adventure area just came. Some of it on a big truck."

"Oh?" She'd expected the bounce house and inflatable slide to go up tomorrow, but the carnival game booths had been erected this morning. "What did you see?"

Annie clutched her hands together. "Lots. The lady with red hair—"

"Miss Gretchen," Wynn corrected.

"Miss Gretchen says me and Wynn and Nora and

Logan can try out some of the play structures if our mommies say it's okay."

It shouldn't stick in her craw that Gretchen used the word *mommy*, because for all intents and purposes, that's what Clementine was to Wynn and Annie. But Brielle was their mother. It would be helpful if Gretchen didn't remind the children they were orphans.

Faith wasn't Nora and Logan's mommy, either. She loved them as her own, but their mother had died a few years ago. Was Gretchen careless, or intending to salt the kids' wounds?

Goodness, Clementine must be tired to have such uncharitable thoughts about Gretchen. Surely, she hadn't meant anything by referring to Clementine and Faith as moms. Gretchen may not be the best of friends with Clementine, and yes, maybe she did sometimes wonder when she wasn't with Liam if he were with Gretchen instead, helping her as he had been when he'd captured the film footage. But Clementine was overreacting.

She handed Liam another set of string lights, eyes on the kids. "What type of play structures?"

"A hay bale maze and a rope thing you crawl across and a horizontal ladder like the one at school—"

"And a playhouse that looks like an old-timey building," Annie interrupted.

"And a ball pit, and some big fake flowers that I'm pretty sure are gonna squirt water at people, but when I asked, Miss Gretchen just shrugged and did this." Wynn mimed zipping his lips closed. "And the twins' dad donated a climbing wall. It's gotta be six stories high."

Liam chuckled. "Maybe two stories."

Clementine couldn't laugh, though. Tom ran an outdoor-gear store, The World Outside, and while his sales floor included a kiddie version of a climbing structure atop a mat that was safe for children to play on, this sounded way more intense.

"I thought the adventure area was for young children."

"All ages, so you can come play, too." Annie's excitement was almost irresistible.

Except to Clementine. She could never get excited about a climbing wall. "I'm almost done here. Wait a few minutes and we can go together."

"But Logan and Nora are waiting. Please, Clemmie?" Annie clasped her chubby hands beneath her chin.

Much as she wanted to go supervise, Clementine couldn't leave Liam. There were still a few packages of light strings to open and hang, and it would be easier and faster if she stayed. "No rope thing unless an adult is watching. And no climbing wall."

"Tomorrow the climbing wall," Annie asserted.

"No, that's not what I meant. Feet on the ground, okay?"

"Let's go tell Logan and Nora!" Wynn bolted back toward the kids' area, Annie at his heels.

"Feet on the ground!"

She prayed they heard her holler. Shaking her head, she glanced up at Liam. "I can't believe Tom got a climbing wall like that. Let's get this finished so I can go supervise."

"I've got a good vantage from here. The kids are avoiding it completely. Going for the maze, feet on the ground, just like you said. You don't need to worry." Liam reached to hang the string on a hook.

Her shoulders tensed. "I'm not being overprotective."

"I didn't say you were, but I know you struggle with anxiety over risky things. I'm not coming down on you for that. Even irrational things can be triggers and set off panic."

Irrational? Had he just said she was irrational?

Her vision clouded. "I don't care what anyone else thinks. It's my job to protect those children. I don't expect you to understand any of my choices, but you said yourself, you don't have kids. And even if you did, you haven't been through what we have. If that makes my rules irrational, so be it."

Liam froze. "I didn't mean *you* were irrational. I meant even when fears are irrational, that doesn't invalidate them. But you're right. I don't know what I'm doing. I'm the last person who knows how to take care of kids."

She hadn't meant to sound so harsh. She'd wanted to make her point, sure, but in her fatigue, she'd gone too far. "Liam, I misunderstood, but even then, I shouldn't have—"

"No, I get it. The only model I had was a dad so obsessed with his art he didn't notice anyone around him and a mom who yelled at the world. So what do I know?" He hooked the string lights. "This is the last one, if you want to go check on the kids."

She did, but she didn't want to leave things like this between them. Her anger had melted to an uneasy pit in her stomach. "I'm sorry for barking at you. This had nothing to do with you at all or your parents. I'm touchy when it comes to risks, as you know, but I shouldn't have snapped."

"Nothing to apologize for. We're good, okay?"

How could they be good? But he was smiling, so she nodded. "Okay."

"I'm sorry you're anxious. Go check on the kids, and then I think we'll be ready for DeLuca's."

"Sounds good." Folding her arms over her chest, she hurried around the hedge.

Parenting was complicated, and her anxieties weren't necessarily unfounded. But was being this anxious what God wanted for her?

Of course not. The Bible was full of passages of comfort and peace for the worried and fearful. She'd memorized a few, thanks to Liam's handwritten card that she'd taped to the bathroom mirror.

God wanted His children to experience His peace, yet she wasn't acting as if that life of peace was available. Or that she even wanted to let go of her fears and grab hold of His promises.

How to do it, though? She didn't know, but stuffing her shaking hands into the front pockets of her sweatshirt, she knew she didn't want to live like this forever.

"My, my." Grandma looped her arm through Liam's so they could walk in tandem through the festival gate the following afternoon. Before them, facades of old-fashioned buildings and volunteers in period costume gave the illusion that the festival visitors had stepped back in time, and fiddle music over the loudspeakers and the mouthwatering scent of roasting meat added a richness to the senses. Liam might be biased, but the team's hard work had paid off.

"I'd have loved this as a kid."

"I love it now, and I haven't been a kid in decades." Grandma squeezed Liam's elbow. "We're barely inside, and it appears Gold Rush Days is already a hit."

"There's certainly a crowd." Liam's shoulders relaxed in relief. He'd been curious how well attended today's grand opening would be, considering it was midafternoon on a Friday and adults with nine-to-five jobs were still at work.

He needn't have given the matter a second thought. Families with strollers and elementary-age kids walked through the gate, wide eyes taking in the scene, while clusters of teenagers viewed the world through their phone screens. Couples wandered hand in hand or clutched the maps he and Clementine had worked on.

All that work was over now. No more maps, schedules, charts, social media posts, phone calls or planning. No more reason to hang out with Clementine and the kids, other than to film her property for her website.

If she still wanted him to, that is. She'd been hard to read last night after he'd stuck his foot in his mouth about irrational fears. Sure, she'd said things were okay, but it didn't feel quite right. He didn't want to leave town with things tense between him and Clementine. They'd become friends, and he didn't want to lose that.

Again.

"You look gloomy."

"Just thinking that you were right, Grandma. Helping with the festival kept me occupied while I recuperated. I'm glad I could do it." He shrugged his left shoulder. It didn't feel great, but it didn't feel awful, either. This was his first night without the sling. At today's doctor appointment, he'd been given permission to go without now.

She eyed him like she knew he wasn't telling the whole truth. "You aren't finished helping, though, are you? You and Clementine have the Gold Star Favorites contest tomorrow. Where is she anyway?"

"I'm not sure. Last night at pizza, the kids asked if I'd join them at some point. I'd like to, if that's okay with you."

"It's more than okay, dear one." Her smile turned sly.

"Not like that, Grandma. As friendly—" he fumbled for a word "—co-committee members."

Grandma snorted. "That's hilarious."

"So are you and Rex."

She sputtered. "What are you talking about?"

"Acting like you're not a thing, but I saw the take-out container in the fridge. The receipt taped to it had his name on it, not yours. You had dinner with him last night, didn't you?"

"Look. It's the kids."

"I'm not falling for that trick, Grandma."

Frowning up at him, she pointed a gnarled forefinger down the asphalt entrance.

Oh. Wynn and Annie rushed toward them, followed by a smiling Clementine.

"Mrs. Murphy. Mr. Liam." Annie patted them on their wrists. "You found us."

"If we don't hurry, there'll be a long line to pan for gold." Wynn had never spoken so fast in Liam's hearing. "You have to help me pan for gold."

Clementine might not want him to, however, after last night. Maybe he'd better give her more space. "I'm sure you've got it all by yourself, though, Wynn."

"But we might strike it rich. Don't you want to, with me?"

Liam doubted there were enough gold flakes in the sluice boxes to buy a sandwich, since the activity was intended for kids and more about the experience than "striking it rich" in a monetary sense. But Wynn was excited and wanted Liam close.

And the last thing Liam wanted to do was say no. "I'd love to, if it's okay with Clementine."

Her gaze was soft. "Join us. Marigold, how about you?"

"Fun as it sounds, I'm parched. Apple cider sounds rather good about now."

Liam followed the direction of her gaze. Rex Rigsby stood in a short line at a cider cart, waving. When he realized Liam watched, his hand fell and he turned away, cheeks reddening. Why were they keeping their relationship a secret? Oh, well. "Enjoy your cider, Grandma. Text me when you're ready to go home."

"Find lots of gold, kids." She hurried off, her white culottes swishing against her calves.

"She forgot to give me a butter mint," Annie lamented.

"Who cares about mints when there's real gold?" Wynn reached for Liam's hand. "Come on."

They made their way to the Old Town area, bypassing one historical guide after another in their hurry to reach the panning-for-gold section.

"Where's your sling?" Clementine glanced at his shoulder.

"My X-ray looked good today. The doctor said I can start full range-of-motion exercises. No weight training for a few more weeks, but otherwise, I'm healing well."

"Don't push it, then."

"By panning for gold?" It was hard not to tease. "Gold might be one of the heavier metals, but I doubt we'll find that much, Clem."

The tug of Wynn's hand drew him back to the task at hand. "We might. There it is."

Thankfully, there wasn't a line yet, and a bearded man in khaki jeans, brogans and a red gingham shirt set the kids up at a sluice box with shallow, round pans.

He demonstrated how to scoop silty water into the pan, swirl, rinse, swirl and check what was left in the pan for gold. "You can keep what you find, but you have to stop once you find gold so others can take a turn."

No matter how hard Liam peered, all he saw in the sluice box was water and nondescript dirt. Not a shiny fleck anywhere. "What if they don't find gold?" he asked over his shoulder.

The bearded fellow responded with a wink.

Wynn, it turned out, was a natural at scooping up soil from the bottom of the sluice box and swirling the silty contents around in his round plastic pan. Annie, however, found it far more fun to treat the pan like a plate in need of a thorough washing. She'd never find any gold that way—

"Wait, Annie. What's that right there?" Clementine's unpainted fingernail tapped a shiny yellow speck in the pan.

"Is that gold?" Annie's voice was awestruck wonder.

"Wow! You're supposed to say 'Eureka,' Annie." Wynn didn't display jealousy but joy for his sister.

"You-reek-a." Annie's eyes were huge.

The bearded guy came back to bottle up Annie's finding and some water in a tiny flask. "Here's your gold, little lady."

"Now it's your turn, Wynn." Liam was determined the boy would soon shout "Eureka," too. "Ready to try again?"

Wynn's enthusiastic nod made the cowlick on the back of his crown wobble. "There's gonna be a nugget in this one."

Swirl, swirl, rinse, swish, repeat. "That's it, bud. You're doing great. Nice and gentle."

"Need me to help?" Clementine hovered behind Wynn.

Liam spared her a hasty glance. "Thanks, but we've got this."

"Yeah. The boys' team's got this," Wynn echoed.

No gold in his pan, though. Wynn tried fresh silt and repeated the process of swishing, swirling, rinsing. Nothing. He tried again. And again.

The boys' team, it seemed, didn't have it down after all. "Where's the gold?" Wynn's frustrated grunt sounded close to a cry.

Liam put a hand on the boy's narrow shoulder. "You're doing great. Just what the man showed us to do." Not that it had mattered in Annie's case, but that was life sometimes. Like Annie, Liam didn't always play by the rules, but things had a way of working out. "Gotta be patient, like the old forty-niners back in the day— Hey there, what's that?"

"Eureka!" Wynn's shout made Liam's ears ring, but he didn't care.

He clapped Wynn's shoulder while the man in the gingham shirt scooped Wynn's gold into a flask. "Look at that. Your patience paid off."

Wynn wrapped one arm around Liam's waist for a short but fierce hug of triumph. "Thanks for your help."

"I didn't do anything."

Clementine's eyes were soft. "Yes, you did, Liam. You did so much for Wynn. Thank you."

The kids' comparisons of their gold flakes and the noise of the festival faded as Liam smiled down at Clementine. Held her gaze.

She was so lovely, so beguiling. As the son of a sculptor, Liam knew a thing or two about art, and Clementine was a masterpiece. He could admire her forever and never grow tired of his view.

He recognized the signs. Knew he should look away, but he couldn't muster the will just yet. He was drawn to stay right here in this moment. Wanted to cup her cheek and trace her lips with his thumb.

Kiss her.

"Clemmie, hold this."

Annie's high voice was a jarring slap of ice water, putting Liam solidly back in his place. Gold Rush Days. With children.

And he and Clementine were not—would not ever be again—like *that*.

Clementine dipped her head, and her hair fell like a veil over her face, so he couldn't read her features. "Why don't I put those flasks in my purse for safe-keeping?"

"I don't want mine getting confused with Annie's."

"Here, yours goes in the front pocket of my purse and Annie's in the back pocket. Now we can tell them apart."

Satisfied, Wynn grinned at Liam. "Since we already found gold, what should we do next?"

Not kiss your aunt, that's for sure.

Just because there wouldn't be kissing didn't mean Liam didn't want to be with Clementine and the kids, though. He was happy right here, with these three people.

His remaining time with them was running short. He was determined to enjoy every moment he could.

Chapter Ten

By early afternoon the next day, Clementine wished she'd worn different shoes for the second day of the festival.

Sure, her turquoise boots were her favorite, complementing her best jeans, white button-down blouse and colorful beaded necklace. But after running around last night with the kids and spending the morning on her feet selling her products at the vendor fair, she wished she'd sneaked a pair of memory-foam slippers into her bag. No one could see her feet behind the table anyway.

Except for Liam, who'd come behind the table to deliver her a hot dog for lunch half an hour ago and hadn't left. Marigold and Rex had come with him, looking mighty cozy to Clementine, and offered to treat the kids to lunch, followed up by a visit to the art fair. She'd readily agreed, knowing the kids would be happier doing something other than the activity books she'd brought for them.

She was also free to focus on her business, but truth be told, it was a struggle to think about sheep-milk soap with Liam beside her.

His dark gaze flickered down to her feet. "Those turquoise boots are something."

Right there, it was worth the discomfort of standing in the boots all day.

"Thanks. Yours are…the same as the ones you wear every day." She laughed.

"Yeah, well, they're comfortable. I don't really have any shoes that go with the whole gold rush theme."

"No 1850s ensembles?" She wolfed down her last bite of hot dog topped with mustard and relish. Liam remembered how she liked them.

"I left them in my closet at the casita," he teased. "Actually, I think the people who dressed up in period garb look great. Faith and Tom, Gretchen, all those historical guides. I filmed a lot of them this morning for next year's festival promotion."

"I'm so glad you could do that. It'll really make the website pop." She wiped mustard off her finger with a napkin.

"Hey, guys." Leah Dean came up to the table, hand in hand with her fiancé, Benton. "I'm in the market for soap."

"You've come to the right place." Clementine reached across the table to hug her friend. They spent a few minutes chatting while Leah and Benton examined the bars.

"Sweet Clementine. Cute name and I love the citrus scent." Leah set aside a few bars. "I liked the Magi one you had at Christmas. Frankincense and myrrh. Ooh, this one's nice, too. Lemongrass. Benton, what do you think?"

Benton sniffed. "I like it. Reminds me of Marigold."

"Grandma is a huge fan of lemongrass, for sure." Liam tapped the stack of Patchouli Cedarwood bars.

"This one's my personal favorite, though. One use, and I was convinced Clementine's soap is better than anything on the market."

Benton investigated the bar. "I'm sold."

Grinning, Leah added three of the cedarwood bars to her purchase pile. "Maybe you should hire Liam, Clementine. He's quite the salesman for Honeysuckle Farms products."

The idea of Liam staying in town both thrilled and terrified Clementine, but it was silly to even think about. He was leaving in a week, and with that impish look in his eyes, he clearly took Leah's joke for what it was. She decided to do the same. "If you stay on, I'll give you a discount on all my products."

He scratched his beard as if considering. "I'll keep it in mind if my day job falls through."

Everyone smiled at his lighthearted comment, but seriously, he deserved thanks for all he'd done to help her. Earlier, he'd overseen the setup for the Gold Star Favorites contest while she manned her table, and even though the day wasn't over yet, she'd earned enough already to make a good start toward the new electric fencing. God had provided. "I really am grateful for all you've done, Liam."

He shook his head. "I haven't done much."

"I disagree, and I appreciate you helping my friend." Leah selected a few bars of Rose Gold soap and some dishwashing scrubbies. "She's one of the hardest-working women I've ever met."

"I would say the same of you." Clementine totaled the order. "Nurse, dutiful granddaughter, house restorer, and now you're on the board for the memory care unit at the retirement village? You're a wonder."

"And she's all mine." Benton kissed Leah's temple.

Clementine had to look away. Benton and Leah shared an unconditional, genuine love. They'd found their way together despite the obstacles they'd faced, and happy as she was for them, Clementine couldn't help but feel…not jealous, but hollow. The only man she'd ever loved was one she could never have.

I ask again for You to take away these feelings, Lord, but if not, please give me the strength to accept them as a reminder to keep turning toward You.

She didn't have time for romance anyway. Not with the kids—

Gia, the frizzy-haired brunette Clementine had hired to cover her for the afternoon, appeared behind Leah, her wide grin gleaming with the sparkle of her orthodontics. "I'm here to relieve you."

"It's that time already?" Clementine checked her watch. Sure enough, the Gold Star Favorites contest was starting shortly. Marigold and Rex were supposed to meet them here at the table five minutes ago. "I wonder where the kids are."

Gia slipped around the table. "I ran into them at the funnel cake stand, and I'm supposed to tell you they'll see you at the food contest. Mrs. Murphy wanted to get good seats."

"After all the walking they've done today, I don't blame them for wanting to take a load off." Liam clapped Benton's shoulder. "This contest is our baby, so we've got to run. See you tomorrow at church."

"Oh, we're heading over to the contest, too." Benton took the bag of products from Clementine. "We're going to drop these off at the first aid station so we don't have to haul them around."

"Thanks for your purchase." Clementine hoisted her cross-body purse over her shoulder before turning to her teenage helper. "And thanks to you, Gia. Any questions before I go?"

"I've helped you at enough farmers' markets that I know the drill. See you after dinner."

Clementine smiled at her as she and Liam left, but she felt her smile slip the moment they'd cleared the vendor fair area. The next few hours would be jam-packed, given the food contest, the pet event and feeding the kids. Thankfully, Bo Peep was settled behind the petting zoo, secure in a straw-filled pen with her brother, Boy Blue, for company. They were undoubtedly missing their mama and the rest of the flock, but otherwise, were they okay?

She jumped when a hand gently touched her shoulder.

"Sorry, didn't mean to scare you." Liam grimaced, hand midair. "You just tensed up and I wasn't thinking, just trying to offer comfort."

"Sorry. Just going over things in my head. It's a busy day."

"But a good one. Don't worry. Rex said he'd look in on the lambs, right? So right now, they're safe, fed and watered, probably snoozing."

Even after all this time, he knew her well enough to suspect her mind was torn between her festival obligations and her animals. "You're right."

"And the kids are fine. Rex and Grandma have been spoiling Wynn and Annie from the sound of things, buying them funnel cakes."

"Speaking of Rex and Marigold, what is going on with those two?" They turned the corner, so they were mere steps from the Gold Star Favorites stage. "He hasn't said a word, but they took the kids together."

"Grandma's not talking, but I'm sure they're dating. They want to keep it quiet for now, I guess." They'd entered the staging area, and his gaze locked on his grandma and Rex, who sat front and center in the viewing area, heads together, while Wynn and Annie sat on either side of the couple, chomping candied apples.

Oh boy. Candied apples and funnel cakes? The upcoming sugar crash would be brutal.

But the kids' sugar consumption and its effects would have to wait, because Mayor Judy Hughes, one of the contest's three judges, paced the stage, mouth set in a grim line, arms folded so tight across her chest it looked like her top half was in danger of snapping off.

Bracing herself, Clementine hurried to the stage to face the mayor's wrath.

Liam's last encounter with the mayor had been when he was about fourteen, eating popsicles with friends on the Fourth of July…while blocking the sidewalk. Judy Hughes hadn't been mayor back then, but she'd given him the same haughty look as she now gave Clementine.

Liam hurried with Clementine to the stage, where two hours ago he'd helped set up three long, portable tables and spread them with red-checkered tablecloths. A few covered dishes left by contestants had already been placed on it, but there was plenty of time before the contest began. Everything seemed in order, so what was the mayor's problem?

The mayor was dressed for the festival in jeans, a yolk-yellow blouse and white blazer, a cowboy hat atop her platinum cropped hairdo. She spun on the toe of her high-heeled boot, shaking a headset microphone at them. "I can't use this."

Hello to you, too. Liam forced a smile. "That microphone wasn't intended for you."

Mayor Hughes dropped the headset onto the food table with a relieved sigh. "Good. I hate those things. Where's the handheld?"

"We don't have another microphone." Clementine's words were slow, cautious. "I'm wearing this one while I emcee the contest."

"That won't work. I need a handheld to address the crowd."

Clementine met Liam's glance before returning her focus to the mayor. "According to the schedule, your only remarks today are the ones you made this morning and the speech before tonight's bluegrass concert. Right now, all you have to do is taste delicious things and pick your top three favorites."

The mayor started shaking her head before Clementine finished talking. "As mayor, I'd like to address my constituents everywhere I go at this silly festival. I need to be front and center."

Liam's vision narrowed. "You will be. As a judge. And the Gold Rush Days isn't silly. Look around at all your constituents, having a good time, with the proceeds going to such a worthy cause."

Clementine nudged him as if to tell him to cool his tone down a fraction. "Your being here is good PR as it is. But if you insist, you're welcome to use the headset before I emcee the contest. I'm happy to share it with you."

Eyes narrowed to slits, the mayor caught sight of

someone and then snapped her fingers. "Faith. Come up here."

Faith, dressed for the festival in a full-skirted green dress that fit into the period of the town's founding, hurried to join them. "Is something the matter?"

"I'll say. You're in charge of this festival, right? I need a microphone." Mayor Hughes mimed holding one. "Fetch one for me."

Faith didn't answer. In fact, her attention had diverted to the woman who ran the yarn store brushing past her with a casserole for the contest table. The dish lacked a lid, and the delicious aroma of a Thai yellow curry swirled around them.

"Faith? Microphone." Mayor Hughes snapped her fingers.

"Um." Faith's lips parted.

"I don't blame you for wanting a sample, Faith." Liam rubbed his stomach. Hopefully, a little humor would lessen the mayor's glower and draw Faith's attention back to the moment.

Faith didn't smile, though. "I can't."

"That's what we were telling the mayor. This is the only microphone we have." Clementine's brow furrowed. "Faith? Are you okay?"

"I don't feel well."

"Is it that same bug from Easter?"

"Not a bug." Faith's hand covered her mouth, but her words were still audible. "Pregnant."

In a blur of green, Faith ran in the direction of the restrooms.

Liam felt like his eyes might bug out of his head. Had she said what he thought she'd said?

Tom, dressed vintage-style in brown pants, a plaid

shirt and suspenders, entered the contest area, scanning for a seat…or his wife. Liam beckoned him up to the stage. "Faith's sick, Tom. Told us she's pregnant and ran out of here. Congratulations."

"Thanks." Tom smiled as he stepped away. "Gotta go find her. This morning sickness thing is a lie—it's all-day sickness."

Clementine had a happy, wistful look on her face. "A baby," she said to Liam. "Much better than a virus."

"Much."

Liam would've cheered for Tom and Faith, but the mayor's glare brought him back to the task at hand. "Sorry, ma'am. If you could please wait over there with the other judges. I'm sure you know Bob, the high school principal, and Bette, principal of WPC Elementary. Thanks for your service."

Maybe she was enticed by the prospect of sampling that aromatic curry, or maybe she realized every eye had been drawn by Faith's rushing out due to morning sickness, but Mayor Hughes obliged without further ado.

In the amount of time it had taken to confer with the mayor, the seats had filled up and a few more dishes had appeared on the table. Time to get this show on the road. Liam covered the entries with silver domes while Clementine assigned each dish a number. He scanned the table. "Are we missing anything?"

"Well, there's the correct number of dishes on the dais, and I see some of our entrants." Clementine consulted her list. "Marge Old and King Biggers were last-minute additions. I have no idea who those people are, but like I said, there are the correct number of entries, so I think we're good to go."

"Let's start the party, then. You've got this, emcee."

Liam stepped back to handle fork duty for the judges while Clementine introduced the contest. Back in their school days, she'd never been one to get up on stage for plays or debates, but this afternoon, she was a natural— clear, concise, with excellent timing. Was her sense of ease with public speaking something she'd grown into? Or had it always been there, but he'd never seen it?

Delighted as he was to watch her, he couldn't help but note the pang of sorrow in his gut. They'd thought themselves so grown up back in high school, knowing exactly what they wanted. Except he'd discounted her desire to grow roots, sure if she joined him on his adventures, she'd be as happy as he was.

He'd been too young and full of himself to accept that they wanted different things. Were different people.

She'd been right to break up with him back then. For so long, he'd resented her decision. But now, it was obvious she'd become who she was supposed to be, and boy, was it a sight to behold. She was confident. Beautiful. She was even lovelier now, if such a thing was possible.

His thoughts were broken by the audience's laughter, oohs and aahs as each dish was tested and tasted. The curry, an apricot pie, corn pudding flecked with red peppers, a creamy rich butternut soup, a golden apple pie, nachos dripping with cheddar cheese sauce, pumpkin soufflé, grilled pineapple spears and— That last one sure looked like Grandma's marmalade cake, with that pool of orange jam on top. She wasn't on the list of entrants, though.

In the audience, Grandma giggled. Liam rolled his eyes. Marge Old. Marigold?

After the tastings finished, Clementine shut off her mic to confer with the judges. Then she flipped the switch back on. "I've been assured by the judges that everything was delicious. I, for one, am envious of them for getting to taste them all. They look and smell amazing, don't they?"

"Except to Faith," Grandma said too loudly.

"I have a feeling she'll be hungry later," Clementine said back. "But for now, I have the honor of announcing the winners. In third place, the apricot pie baked by Maude Donalson. Maude, come on up here for your ribbon."

Maude, Grandma's friend with the peach-colored hair, stomped up the stage steps. "This is a blue-ribbon pie, I'll have you know."

"It was a tough choice for the judges," Liam assured her. "I think it was very close."

"I'd imagine so." Maude grabbed the third-place ribbon and crossed her arms.

"Second place," Clementine continued on, "is the corn pudding. The winner is King Biggers. King, would you come up for your ribbon?"

The crowd gasped and gaped when Rex stood up. "I thought a pseudonym was in order."

Rex meant *king*, didn't it? *Very funny, Rex and Grandma.*

Unlike Maude, Rex beamed and waved the ribbon at Marigold and the kids.

"You told me you can't cook," Clementine said, making the audience laugh.

"He can't," shouted an older fellow in the back.

"I took a class with a friend." Rex's lips twitched.

"I can guess who that friend is. We're going to have to talk about this later." Clementine held up her note card. "But right now, it's my honor to announce that first place in our first Gold Rush Favorites contest goes to the marmalade cake by Marge Old."

"That's me." Grandma hopped up, clapping. "See what we did with our names, there?"

Liam squeezed her shoulders. "Nice job, Marge."

"We feel so sneaky." She held up her ribbon to the audience. "Thank you, judges."

"Yes, a hearty round of applause for our judges and for all the contestants. Everything looked wonderful." As folks clapped, Clementine gestured for Wynn and Annie to join her on the stage. Annie grabbed Clementine's legs, but Wynn ran straight to Liam.

"It's almost time for the pet show. You're coming with us, aren't you?"

Liam clapped Wynn's narrow shoulder. "I wouldn't miss it."

Wynn beamed, but Annie's lower lip protruded. "I want a bite of ma-ma-lade cake first."

"The food up here is not for us." Clementine smoothed Annie's wispy hair. "Besides, you've had enough sweets. Candied apples and funnel cakes?"

Rex whistled and looked away as if innocent.

Wynn's smile fell and he scuffed the toe of his boot into the stage floor. Liam returned his hand to the boy's shoulder. "Are you nervous about the pet show?"

Wynn shrugged.

"It's okay to be nervous, if you are."

"Do you ever get nervous?"

"Oh yeah. Some situations are nerve-wracking, plain and simple. Like taking a test or making a speech. I couldn't have done what Clemmie did just now, talking in front of all those people." He glanced at Clementine, who congratulated Maude on her pie.

Come to think of it, just looking at her made him nervous sometimes, because if he wasn't careful, he was never going to get over his feelings for her.

Liam refocused on Wynn, glad the boy was confiding in him. "You remember this isn't a contest, right? No winning or losing, because all the pets are precious to their owners."

"Yeah, but if someone asks me about her and I don't know the answer, I don't want to make Bo Peep look bad."

"Impossible. One glance at Bo Peep and everyone will see what great care you and Annie take of her. If you forget that, though, and your nerves threaten to get the best of you, just remember God is with you."

"I wish I could see Him sometimes."

Liam could relate. "We have to trust He's there, just like He promised."

Wynn's arms wrapped around Liam's waist, and a warm feeling swelled in Liam's chest. *I hope I've helped him, God. I'd never want to hurt these kids.*

"Are you two ready to see Bo Peep?" Clementine had Annie by the hand, her curious gaze flickering from Wynn to Liam.

"We're ready." Wynn released Liam only to reach for his hand.

It felt small, hot, a little sticky and better than Liam ever imagined holding a child's hand could feel. Like he was someone special in this little boy's life. His heart swelled twice its size and puffed out his chest.

"Liam, there you are."

The female voice behind him was as familiar to him as Grandma's. He spun around. "Sara, what are you doing here?"

His sister hadn't indicated she had any intention of visiting sometime soon. This clearly wasn't a mere family visit, though. Her dark-eyed gaze locked on to his face, full of agony.

She grabbed his left shoulder, causing pain to his still-tender collarbone. "I didn't know where else to go, and you're the only person who gets it. I wish I'd done what you did, just kiss love goodbye and live for yourself."

Chapter Eleven

"I'm so sorry," Sara wailed, head in her hands, her long dark hair hiding her face. "I didn't even notice them, and I've probably scarred those kids for life. See? I have no business being a mother."

Liam leaned forward on the metal folding chairs where he and Sara sat in the now-empty stage area. "Wynn and Annie were so excited to get their lamb dolled up for the pet show, I don't think they paid any attention to what you said."

But Clementine had heard and understood. Her jaw had gone slack, and she'd pulled Wynn from Liam's hold. He was only able to offer a quick promise that he'd be at the pet show before she hauled the kids away, fast. Grandma had made a beeline for Sara, but his sister had asked for time alone with Liam, so Grandma had gone off with Rex, her face stricken with worry.

Sara lifted her head and pushed her long, straight hair from her face. "My timing's terrible. You're missing out on that dog show thing. Or maybe you're grateful I'm giving you an excuse not to go. You're not exactly the kiddie-stuff type."

Then, he'd changed, because he really wished he were with the kids right now, taking pictures of them and Bo Peep. In fact, it was hard to not harbor a negative feeling or two toward his sister's timing as well as what she'd said within the kids' earshot.

"It's important to me to support Wynn and Annie, but I'm worried about you. What brought you all the way to Widow's Peak Creek, unannounced?"

"Compromise doesn't work." She rolled her dark eyes.

"You knew when you got married that you were becoming a team, Sara. You committed to Dane. Your marriage."

"I didn't think the team members would turn out to want such different things. I thought if we loved each other, we'd always be on the same page."

"I'm proof that's not true."

"Yeah, but you and Clementine were young. That wasn't really love."

The implication he never really loved Clementine raised his hackles, but that wasn't the issue right now. Sara and Dane's marriage was. "I don't think any two people are ever on the same page, love or not. And for what it's worth, Mom and Dad loved each other."

Sara snorted through her tears. "No, they didn't. She was always saying how they didn't fit into each other's worlds, remember?"

"I'm not saying there wasn't a lot of other stuff going on, too, but there was love. You could see it in Dad's sculptures of her. And the way Mom cared for him when he was dying. But yeah, something went sideways along the road, and they didn't let love rule their decisions, that's for sure." Liam stretched out his legs. "I'm not saying what you should do, Sara. The decision to have kids is huge, and you're right, there's no way to both get what you want with this one. But I'm here for you and your marriage."

"My marriage? When did you become Mister Matrimony?"

"I was never against marriage. But after what happened with Clementine, I got to a point where I decided it wasn't what I wanted for myself."

"That sounds past tense." Sara's eyes narrowed. "Have you changed your mind?"

"No, but we're not talking about me right now."

"I never thought of someone caring about my marriage other than me, that's all." She glanced at her smart watch. "I don't want you to miss that pet thing if it's important to you."

"Wynn and Annie are important, so yeah, it is. You and I have seen enough of adults forgetting kids' priorities."

"Like the time they forgot you had photography entries in the county fair. Well, Mom didn't forget, but she was trying to prove a point that Dad forgot, so neither showed up." Sara stood. "You're right. We can talk about my marital woes later. Might not hurt me to get distracted by a dog contest."

"It's not a contest. We walk through the hall and look at people's pets, like a parade in reverse. And it's not just dogs. Bo Peep is a lamb."

The topic of Clementine's sheep dairy was enough to distract Sara, and they got in the line that trailed from the event hall out to the warm asphalt courtyard outside. Sara whistled. "Who knew pets would be such a big deal?"

Liam had a hunch. Pets never failed to lighten moods, entice smiles and bring people together. Hopefully, these animals would cheer Sara up for a few minutes, too. The line was long, but moved fast, and soon enough they were inside the air-conditioned event hall.

The large room reminded Liam of a school cafeteria, with its yellow-splotched linoleum floors and bare white walls that rebounded the noises of conversations along with barks and caws. The air sparked with excitement as well as the faint odors of straw, feed and wet dog. Every face was smiling, and up ahead, he could see Grandma and Rex visiting the last table before the exit door.

Close to the end was Bo Peep's table. Tempted as he was to skip the other pets and rush there, Liam led Sara slowly past table after table, pausing to greet pet owners and admire their fur babies—or feathered or scaled babies, as the case might be, in cages, crates, tanks or held in arms. They viewed parakeets, a cockatoo, hamsters, a fair number of dogs and a tortoise munching a lettuce leaf.

Sara's face lost its strained look, which was nice to see.

It was also nice to introduce Sara to his new friends. Eileen and Trudie, who oversaw the event. The Santos twins, Nora and Logan, shared their cat and dog under the supervision of their doting grandma since Tom was staying with Faith while her stomach settled. Joel Morgan and his stepdaughter, Maisie, were positioned right beside Wynn and Annie. After winking at Clementine and the kids, he introduced Sara to the Morgans, then gestured to the gray flop-eared rabbit in Maisie's arms. "What's your bunny's name?"

"Fluff, because he's the softest thing ever." Maisie's voice was soft as she looked up at him through her pink-rimmed glasses. "Want to pet him?"

Joel chuckled. "You should. Trust me."

Annie left her table to sidle beside Maisie, running her hand down the rabbit's back. "He's softer than Bo Peep. Do it like this, Mr. Liam."

"All right." Liam stroked the bunny down the spine. The gray fur was smooth as silk. "You're right, ladies. That is one soft rabbit. Sara?"

His sister didn't stop with one pat. She rubbed an ear, too. "Softest thing ever."

Liam smiled at Maisie. "Thank you for sharing him with us, Maisie."

"Thanks for stopping." Joel's nod indicated that he knew Liam's heart lay elsewhere, but he appreciated the attention given to his little girl.

"Nice to meet you." Sara's smile faltered when they moved to stand in front of Clementine and the kids. "Hi, everyone. I'm sorry for being so rude earlier."

"No worries." Clementine reached across the table to hug Sara. "Good to see you again. I hope everything's all right."

"It'll be fine. So, this must be your niece and nephew?"

Clementine made the introductions, and never shy, Annie gestured to the lamb in Wynn's arms. "This is Bo Peep and she was in her crate, but she's tired of it now so Wynn's giving her a hug."

"She looks fantastic, you guys." Liam whipped out his phone and took photos of the kids with their lamb, who looked sweet with the baby-pink bow around her neck. He took another series of shots of the whole family, with Clementine between the kids. All the while, Wynn and Annie shared tidbits about Bo Peep and East Friesian sheep with Sara.

"Would you take a photo of Bo Peep alone, for the website?" Clementine's blue eyes flashed like crystals. "I'm taking your advice, creating fun bios for the ewes to post online. I want to include a bio for Bo Peep, too."

"My pleasure." Liam took about ten, gratified Clementine liked his idea. "Bo Peep's bio can include the fact that she's acting as farm ambassador today."

She chuckled. "I can see it now. 'Ambassador of Honeysuckle Farms to the Gold Rush Days festival, renowned beauty and snugglebug. Hobbies include grazing, chasing her brothers and sampling gourmet delicacies like tender blackberry canes.' It might be more creative writing than the journalism I'd planned to do once upon a time, but hey."

"You've always been a fantastic writer, Clementine. What a great way to incorporate that into your business."

"You're holding up the line, bro," Sara muttered.

"You're welcome to come around with us if you'd like to stay a little longer." Clementine gestured around the long row of tables.

"Sure." Sara shrugged, leading the way.

Her affirmative answer surprised Liam, but he was glad she'd agreed. He couldn't get enough of the kids' excitement, and if Wynn was still nervous, it didn't show.

Once behind the tables, Liam nudged Clementine's arm with his. "So cute."

"She is, isn't she? We gave her a bath."

"Not Bo Peep. The kids. They're in their element."

She rocked on her bootheels. "I think so, but I'm biased."

"Maybe I am, too, but they're rocking it."

He felt the tug of his sister's gaze. "What?"

"You used the word *cute*. Are you sure you're my globe-trotting, bachelor brother?"

Whatever. "*Cute* is a perfectly valid word right now. Cute pets, cute kids."

"Agreed. They're all cute." Clementine flashed him a smile that disintegrated his ability to think. Until Sara nudged him again.

"Dude, you're into this."

So what if he was? Clementine and the kids were his friends, and friends supported one another. And if a town festival wasn't his usual weekend gig, well, there wasn't anything wrong with that, was there? Maybe it was his spiritual growth, or maybe it was a combination of that and his time in Widow's Peak Creek, but he'd changed in small ways, all for the better. If he was a little more aware of kids and their needs, that was a good thing.

If only he'd changed when it came to his feelings for Clementine, though. He still suffered a weakness for her flashing eyes and wide, beguiling smile.

"Mr. Liam, Wynn's talking to you." Annie patted his wrist.

"Sorry. Lost in thought." Liam fixed his gaze on Wynn. "What'd you say, buddy?"

"Are you eating dinner with us? We're getting barbecue from a food truck."

Liam looked to Clementine for her approval, then Sara. "What do you say?"

"I love barbecue." Sara pulled her cell phone from

the colorful satchel hanging over her shoulder. "I'll text Grandma so she can find us."

"No need. There they are now." Liam waved to Grandma and Rex, who'd just come back in through the entrance. The event was winding down, and the sounds of chatter and the occasional bark were replaced by the scrapes and clanks of metal crates being moved for the pets' transport home.

The older couple approached the table, and Rex hitched his thumb over his shoulder. "I'll get the lambs back with their mama and see to the milking tonight, Clementine. That way you and the kids can stay and enjoy the evening."

Her brow furrowed as she took Bo Peep from Wynn and eased her into the carrying crate. "I couldn't ask you to do that, Rex. You and Marigold should stay and have fun."

Grandma rolled her eyes. "The truth is, we're tuckered out and have had our fill of greasy carnival food. We're ready to call it a day."

While Rex assisted Clementine with the lambs, Grandma hugged everyone, saving the kids for last. They shared a whispered exchange that elicited smiles from all.

What were they talking about? Maybe the fun they'd had eating their way through the sugary treats sold at the festival. Since Wynn and Annie lacked grandparents in town, it was nice that Grandma spoiled them a little bit. As of yet, Grandma didn't have any great-grandchildren from Liam and Sara's cousins.

But when the kids looked straight at him and giggled, he had a sinking feeling that they hadn't been talking about candied apples and funnel cakes.

Chapter Twelve

Clementine tugged a package of cleansing wipes from her purse. Somehow, sauce from Annie's dinner of pit beef and baked beans had ended up all over her chin and cheeks. "What a full day we've had."

Annie's full cheeks jiggled at Clementine's gentle dabbing. "Bo Peep made a lot of people smile because she's so cute. I liked Fluff, though, too."

"Me, too. I don't think I've ever patted a rabbit before." Liam stretched his legs, bumping Clementine's under the table. He jerked them back. "Sorry."

"No worries. I hardly felt it."

Well, that wasn't quite true. It hadn't hurt. The bump was more of a brush than a kick. But it had nevertheless sent a jolt up Clementine's leg bones, and now a hot blush crept up her neck. Why was she acting like a middle schooler? As discreetly as she could, she patted her nape with the remnants of the damp wipe she'd used on Annie and grasped to say something to make it seem like she wasn't affected by something as ridiculous as Liam's leg grazing hers.

"Fluff is supercute." It was the most coherent thing she could think of to say.

"Good thing it wasn't a cutest pet contest today, because Fluff is about the same in cuteness as Bo Peep." Wynn wiped his mouth with his napkin.

"Agreed." Sara scooped baked beans with her spork. "But I liked that tortoise, too. Goes to show beauty is in the eye of the beholder."

"I don't know what that means, but Clemmie says our love makes our animals beautiful to us." Wynn bit into his corn, spurting juice.

"It means about the same thing," Liam said, glancing at Clementine. "Love changes how we look at things."

Oh, no. Here came that hot blush again. *You are being such a dummy. He's talking about pets. Not you.*

"Clemmie?" Annie patted her hot cheek.

Great. Now Annie was going to ask why Clementine was all red.

"Do you think Mommy and Daddy would think Bo Peep is cute, too?"

The heat of Clementine's blush and all thoughts of her own tangled issues dissipated under a rush of affection. Pulling Annie beneath the shelter of her arm, she prayed for wisdom. "I'm sure they'd think she's supercute, and they'd be proud. Not just of Bo Peep, but you and Wynn. You did such a good job today."

"I knew your mom and dad, you know." Liam looked down at Wynn, who was seated beside him. "Your mom baked the best chocolate chip cookies and let me eat them if your aunt and I washed all the dishes."

"And Daddy?" Wynn leaned against Liam's right side.

Liam extricated his arm and wrapped it around

Wynn's narrow shoulders. "He could fix anything. Once, I came by the house to pick up your aunt for a football game and would you believe my car wouldn't start up again? I'm glad your dad was there, because he took one look under the hood, saw what needed to be tightened and fixed it."

"I remember that happening," Sara added. She was the same age as Brielle…or, rather, the age Brielle would have been if she'd lived.

Clementine spent so much time grieving her loss. Brad's, too. Their deaths were fresh in her mind at odd times but also whenever risk factored into a decision. Their opting to break the ski resort's rules and go off trail affected every choice of Clementine's now.

But these stories about Brad and Brielle weren't things she'd thought of in a while. "I remember, too." Not just the car breaking down, though, but other things. Like how Brielle had helped her pick out her clothes for her date and sprayed her with a squirt of her expensive, department store perfume. Brad had been kind to Liam, who was nervous since he'd just received his driver's license.

How many of these stories had she kept alive for the kids? Not enough. She grinned at Wynn across the table. "We invited your mommy and daddy to the football game with us, but they couldn't go, because they had to chase down a goat."

"A goat?" Wynn's face scrunched up. "I thought the only pet you had as a kid was a dog named Candy."

"It wasn't our goat. It was our neighbor's. They had a big field with a lot of animals, including two goats— these neighbors are the ones who got your mom and dad thinking about dairy sheep, but that's another story.

Anyway, the billy goat got out, and oh, he was something." Clementine shuddered. "He'd put his head down and butt into you if you were in the wrong place at the wrong time."

"Like Scooter." Annie giggled.

Liam snapped his fingers. "I remember that goat. What was his name? Tank?"

"Yes, Tank. And oh boy, did he live up to his name when he hit your daddy's backside. See, your mom and dad didn't find Tank. Tank found them."

The kids' belly laughs were contagious, and by the time she finished her story, even Sara wiped tears of laughter from her eyes. "I never heard that part of the story."

"Me, neither," Annie said, which made them all laugh again. Then Annie patted Clementine's arm. "Since we're done eating dinner, we should go to the adventure area again."

"I wish we could, honey, but Gia is expecting me back at the vendor fair in a few minutes. There's still a little time left for me to sell some product, so I need to do that. Then I have to pack up everything that's left and get it to the car." There was a bluegrass concert tonight, too, but she wasn't sure the kids could last that long. They'd had a big day and might be too tired.

"But you need to come." Annie tugged Clementine's hand. "You and Mr. Liam have to get to the middle of the maze."

"Didn't you run through the maze with Mrs. Murphy and Mr. Rex?"

Wynn looked like he'd been caught in a fib. "Yeah, but we want you and Mr. Liam to see it."

Liam rubbed his shoulder as if his collarbone ached,

but he seemed fine enough. "I tell you what. If Clemmie says okay, Sara and I can go with you to the adventure area so Clemmie can work. We'll keep superclose eagle eyes on you guys. Then she can meet us when she's done. Is that fine with everyone?"

Sara gave a thumbs-up. "I'd love to see the maze. Haven't done anything like that in years."

"No, it needs to be Clemmie with you." Wynn's mouth set.

"I have to work now, honey. I'm sorry." Clementine hated to disappoint them, but she needed every dollar she could get in sales today. Once she paid for the electric fencing, then she could finally start accounts for the kids' futures. "You can go to the adventure area with Liam and Sara or stay with me and work on your coloring books."

"Adventure area," the kids said at the same time.

"I want to climb the wall," Annie added.

Not this again. "You guys are too young for that."

Wynn shrugged. "Nora and Logan did it."

"So did Maisie. And Joshua from my class." Annie made her most adorable, endearing face. "Please, Clemmie? We'll be so careful."

"Yeah. I don't want to fall and break something." Wynn shook his head.

Oh boy. She met Liam's solemn gaze. He wasn't judging her, but she could read in the depths of his dark eyes an acknowledgement of how hard this might be for her. He'd offered to watch the kids carefully. Maybe he was right, and she was a tad too overprotective. She wanted to keep the kids safe, but was she going too far?

It had felt so good to remember fun times with Brielle and Brad and tell stories about them. She needed to focus more on their lives—and the lives of their kids—than their deaths. Letting the kids climb a wall, with Liam and Sara supervising, would be a step forward.

She threw up her hands. "Okay. You can climb the wall, but not too high."

Liam held up his hand. "A few feet, tops."

"I'll watch like a hawk." Sara said. "But I hope we can get into that maze."

"I'll take you," Wynn said in a low, fast voice, "but you have to promise that when Clemmie comes, we leave her and Mr. Liam alone in the middle. We told Mrs. Murphy we would."

"I beg your pardon, mister?" Clementine wasn't sure she'd heard correctly, but it seemed like Sara had heard the same thing, based on the way Sara's lips pressed together like she was holding back a laugh. Did Sara know what a relentless matchmaker her grandma was?

Annie took Liam's hand. "Come on, let's go."

"I'll catch up in a second," Sara said. "Just want to say a word to Clementine."

Clementine's stomach swooped. The last time she was alone with Sara, the conversation hadn't gone well. And if Sara wanted to revisit the topic, Clementine wasn't sure this was a discussion she wanted to have.

Now that the kids and Liam were gone, Clementine took a deep breath. "What's up, Sara?"

"The past, as in dredging it up. I had no idea you and Liam were so cozy again."

"We're not cozy."

Sara quirked a disbelieving brow. "So there's nothing—"

"He's helping me out with some things. We're kind

of friends again, but our lives are too different, just like your mom told me sixteen years ago."

Sara puffed out a breath. "That conversation is what I wanted to talk about. My mom and I never should have interfered in your relationship."

"You were right, though." Clementine cleared the paper dinner plates and tossed them into the trash. "Liam couldn't be wholly who he was unless I let him go."

"The truth is, no one knows what could've happened if we hadn't urged you to break up with him. I'm sorry. I hope you can forgive me for butting in back then."

"Of course." It was a long time ago. The scars were still there, but Clementine didn't want to be the type of person who held grudges. Life was too precious to spend it being angry.

After a quick hug, Sara rushed to meet up with Liam and the kids. Clementine returned to the vendor fair, paid Gia and evaluated what was left of her product. "Whoa."

Every bar of Sweet Clementine and Lemongrass had sold, and she only had a few bars each left of the other scents. The dish scrubbies, dryer balls and other wool products had been picked over, as well. She wouldn't have much to pack up to take home—and it sure looked like she'd have enough to pay for the new electric fence.

Fergus couldn't get on her about her sheep escaping after that.

The crowd was thinner now than earlier in the day, but Paige and Kellan Lambert approached her table. Kellan held their baby, Poppy, who sucked her fist.

"Is it too late?" Paige eyed the table. "We've been

busy with the book fair, but I had to come by your table and Maude's before the vendor fair closes."

"Here's what I have left, but I have more product at home and can bring it to church tomorrow. How was the book fair, by the way?"

"Excellent. The proceeds are being split between the town museum and the Veterans Affairs library in Pinehurst, and we'll have good checks to give both of them."

That made sense. Kellan was an army veteran, and he was also opening a second location of his bookstore in Pinehurst.

"So exciting." Clementine bagged Paige's selections.

"Clementine? Oh, Clementine."

At the frantic tone of Sara's voice, Clementine's blood iced. "What happened?"

"It's not bad, okay? But Liam said I should get you. It's Annie."

"Go," Kellan said, stepping around the table. "We'll pack this up and drop it on your porch."

"Thank you." She had the foresight to grab her purse before she joined Sara. "What happened, though, Sara? Please."

"I'm so sorry, Clementine. But she fell."

Chapter Thirteen

By the time Clementine and Annie got back to Honeysuckle Farm from the emergency room, it was eleven o'clock, past both of their usual bedtimes. After parking by Liam's rental car, Clementine unbuckled Annie from her car seat and lifted the drowsy child into her arms. Annie's new cast felt hard and foreign against Clementine's chest.

"Clemmie?"

"We're home now, little one. In a minute you'll be in snuggled up in your pajamas."

Liam waited beneath the porch light, his eyebrows slanted down in concern. "How's the patient?"

"Sleepy." She'd already texted him and Marigold that Annie had broken her forearm. "Everyone else went home?"

"Grandma got sleepy after Wynn went to bed, so Sara drove her home. Rex left soon after and said to tell you the sheep are fine. So are the dogs."

"That's good to hear." At least she didn't have to worry about anything else tonight.

"Hi, Mr. Liam." Annie's voice was thick with sleep. She stuck out her arm. "See my cast?"

Liam tapped the fluorescent-pink cast covering Annie's left elbow to wrist. "Nice color choice."

"It's different than yours. Mine's hard."

"Yeah, braces like mine are softer, but they do a different job than casts."

"We can talk more about it in the morning, okay?" Clementine kissed the top of Annie's head. "Thanks again, Liam. I appreciate you staying with Wynn."

"I'll wait for you to put her to bed, if you don't mind."

Clementine nodded and carried Annie to her room. After she assisted Annie into her pajamas, said nighttime prayers, and exchanged good-night kisses, she gave Annie's hand the *I-love-you* hand squeezes. She checked in on Wynn, too, and kissed his forehead. He slept soundly, mouth open, arms flung wide. To be young again and sleep without worry or care. She watched him breathe for a few moments, listening to the stillness of the evening, the gentle creaks of the house settling, Martha's soft snores as she curled at the foot of Wynn's bed and a cricket chirping out the window.

If only her heart were as peaceful.

Liam waited in the family room. "What can I do for you? A cup of herbal tea? Glass of water?"

"I don't need anything." Except for him to leave.

"Maybe tomorrow, we can all sign Annie's cast, if you think she'd like it."

Clementine's head pounded. "I appreciate you trying to normalize it for Annie, but I don't think this should be treated lightly."

"I'm not." His lips parted in surprise. "But I don't

want to scare her, either. These things happen. Kids take tumbles."

"She didn't tumble. She fell off the horizontal ladder and broke her arm." How ironic, because Clementine hadn't been concerned by the playground-type structures in the adventure area. Only the climbing wall. "It proves the point I've been making all along. Some of these so-called 'appropriate' things for kids are not okay, plain and simple. It's my fault for letting this happen."

Confusion etched Liam's face. "I was the one in charge. It's my fault."

"No, it's mine." Clementine sank onto the couch, staring at the toy-strewn coffee table. "I say no to everything that could hurt them. But tonight, I thought, okay, maybe I've been a little strict. Maybe Brad and Brielle wouldn't want their kids to be told no all the time. Boy, the joke's on me now."

"Because you trusted me?" Hurt laced his tone.

"That's not what I meant." She rubbed her temples. "This could've happened to anyone, Liam. But I'm the one who allowed it to be a possibility. I ignored the risk and said okay."

He sat beside her on the couch. "You can't protect them all the time, though, Clementine. I can't imagine how hard it is to be a parent, but we follow God. That means we have to trust Him."

"There's a difference between trusting God and forgoing common sense. I have to do my part, too, to be cautious so I'm around to raise Wynn and Annie. To protect them. They have to learn to be careful. I don't want them to grow up and—"

"Be like me."

She hated it, but she couldn't lie. "You're so talented, Liam. I'm in awe of what you do, but the risks you take frighten me. I'm sorry to be so blunt. It's been a long day and I'm exhausted and worried and sad and feel like an utter failure."

"Blunt is good. It's honest, at least. And it's nothing I didn't know deep down anyway. You've always cared about me, but there's a limit. I figured that out when you broke up with me right after my dad died. Right before my mom yanked me away from everything familiar. I needed your support then, more than ever, but you didn't let me finish grieving before you dealt me another blow."

She'd hurt him. So much more than she'd guessed at the time. "Much as I wanted to comfort you, to be comforted by you, when all those awful things happened, I didn't want to hold you back. You were already looking toward a future I could never fit into."

He stilled. "Fit into. That sounds like my mom talking." When Clementine didn't respond for a moment, Liam stood up. "You're not denying it. What did my mother have to do with this?"

Well, the cat was out of the bag now. Probably for the best, after sixteen years. "She and Sara talked to me about all the things you wanted to do with your life and how there was no way to compromise and both get what we wanted. No middle ground. I hated to admit it, but they were right. A clean break would make it easier for you to get into a groove at your new school, and sure enough, you landed on your feet. Your life turned out exactly how you wanted. Travel. Adventure. You can't say I'm wrong, can you?"

He turned away. "I guess not."

"Not that it matters, but our breakup hurt me, too. I wish I'd handled it better, though."

"It's not like there's a good way to break up with the person who wanted to spend their life with you."

"You wanted to spend your life with me?" Clementine's eyes blurred with tears. "What did that mean to you? You'd have given up the life you wanted to settle down like I wanted? Or did you think I'd give up what I wanted to be with you?"

Ah, there it was, a flash in his eyes that told her. Back then, he'd thought he'd convince her to join him. To give up her dreams of a quiet home life.

"Our hurting each other was inevitable, then." A hot tear slipped down her cheek. "I did the right thing, cutting it off when I did."

The ringing of Liam's cell phone couldn't have come at a worse time.

He had so much more to say, so many questions to ask. His mom and sister had encouraged Clementine to break up with him? How could they do that to him? They'd known how he felt about her.

Did it even matter now, after so much had happened? Meanwhile, the ridiculous tone kept chirping.

Clementine swiped the lone tear from her cheek. "You should answer it."

"Whoever it is can wait."

"It's kind of late for a social call. What if Marigold needs you?"

Her mention of Grandma's name changed his mind. He lifted his phone, but it wasn't Grandma's name on the screen. "It's Javier, the guy I work with a lot."

"At this hour? Take the call." She strode into the kitchen.

Liam tapped his phone screen and lifted the phone to his ear. "Javi? Everything okay?"

"More than okay, dude." It might be nearing midnight, but Javier sounded as energetic as if he'd just downed an espresso. "We landed the Indonesia gig."

"That's excellent, man." It was a large project that would lead to even bigger contracts for Javier's company. "Happy for you."

"Happy for you, too. Get ready for pink sand beaches, because we fly out in less than two weeks. I need you in the production office Wednesday. I know you're still on sick leave, but you'll be good by the time we go, right? 'Cause if you're not, I have to bring in someone else. Nothing personal, but you know how this works."

Liam did. He was Javier's first choice, but he was replaceable. Liam had learned a long time ago he couldn't say no without there being a cost to his career.

He'd thought he'd have more time in Widow's Peak Creek, though. More time for his collarbone to heal before he had to think about work. He'd planned to spend the time with Grandma...

And Clementine and the kids.

What she'd said though, earlier? Her words had echoed Sara's regarding her situation with Dane. Sometimes, there was no way for two people to meet in the middle, was there? Some things were impossible to compromise on.

He had feelings for Clementine—whether they were new or remnants of the past, he couldn't untangle—but that didn't change anything. They wanted different things out of life, and Clementine's anxiety issues were only exacerbated by Liam's presence in her life. Annie's arm wouldn't have broken if Liam hadn't encouraged Clementine to give in.

He wandered into the kitchen and met Clementine's wide-eyed gaze. She was as still as a sculpture, her beautiful features set in sharp relief from the fluorescent kitchen lights overhead. No sculptor on earth, though, could fully capture the pain reflecting from her eyes.

A clearing throat on the other end of the line demanded his attention. "Liam, you there?"

"Yeah. Sorry. Sure. I'll see you then."

"I knew you wouldn't let me down." Insisting Liam meet him first thing Wednesday morning, Javi signed off.

Clementine turned away, no longer a sculpture as she wiped the counter with a dishrag. "You've got a new assignment?"

He didn't want to part like this, but it was just as well. There was no use prolonging the inevitable. "Indonesia. I have to leave Tuesday."

"Earlier than expected." Her tone was flat.

"I haven't forgotten my promise to film your property for your website, though."

"You don't need to do that. It wasn't even a promise. It was an offer."

"It's something I want to do before I go. I have plans with Grandma tomorrow, but can I swing by midafternoon Monday, so Wynn's home from school? Does three o'clock work? I want to tell the kids goodbye properly. If you don't mind, that is."

She shook her head. "They'd be upset if you left without saying anything."

"I'll be here, then. Good night." He let himself out.

Now will I be free of this lingering tie to her, Lord? Liam started the car for the familiar drive back to the tiny house without any relief to his emotional pain. *Sixteen years is long enough to feel this awful ache over Clementine, isn't it?*

Maybe tomorrow the ache would be less, though. And even less the day after. Until one day, maybe he'd think of Clementine and feel nothing at all, good or bad.

Driving home, though, he wasn't sure if the thought of that day relieved or terrified him.

Chapter Fourteen

Clementine hardly slept that night. Instead of going to church on Sunday, she was stuck repairing a large section of fence between her house and Fergus's, where the wood post had fallen over. The damage made no sense. She and Rex had checked the fences so often it felt like it was all they did lately. Liam had mentioned the possibility of sabotage with her garden fence, but who would do that to her? And why? Nothing had been stolen or vandalized.

If this was sabotage, it was like a series of paper cuts. Painfully annoying, distracting but nothing that would send her to her knees.

Then there was the matter of telling the kids Liam was leaving earlier than planned. She waited until after they'd watched the prerecorded livestream of church after dinner Sunday evening.

"But he'll be back, right?" Wynn's thin eyebrows puckered.

"To visit, but I don't know when." She had to tell them the truth, even though it wasn't what they wanted to hear. "When he's not traveling for work, he lives in another city. He was only in Widow's Peak Creek to visit Mrs. Murphy."

Annie scrambled onto Clementine's lap, her cast bumping Clementine's arm. "But he has to live here so he can be our uncle."

Wynn gaped. "You weren't supposed to tell, Annie."

"I don't care." Annie's face reddened. "Mrs. Murphy thinks he should stay, too, and that's why he and Clemmie were supposed to go into the maze where it's romantic-y."

Something snapped in Clementine's brain. With everything that had happened since Annie broke her arm, she'd forgotten about that odd exchange on Saturday night. The kids had wanted her and Liam to be alone in the center of the maze. There'd also been that bit of conspiratorial giggling with Marigold. Had they become minimatchmakers?

"I'm sorry, but Mr. Liam can't be your uncle. He's our friend, but that's all."

No wonder Clementine didn't sleep much Sunday night, either, for thinking about the kids wanting her and Liam to…never mind. Between that, Annie being cranky over the pain in her arm and the idea that her fences were being cut on purpose, she was so overwhelmed she was close to tears Monday afternoon when Liam pulled into her driveway.

She'd rather he didn't see her cry. Turning her head away, she took a few deep breaths.

God, I need Your strength.

"Mr. Liam." Wynn ran past her, tailed by his grinning little sister. "You made it."

"Wouldn't have missed this. How's your arm, Annie?"

"Okay, I guess. Clemmie gave me medicine and I took a nap with Martha on the couch yesterday."

"Naps are good. You have to take it easy when you break a bone. Take it from me." Liam laughed.

More composed, Clementine turned back. Liam retrieved a case from the trunk of his car. "I brought the drone. We're going to have some fun with this."

"No touching unless Mr. Liam says it's okay." Clementine met them halfway on the drive. "Thanks again for this, Liam."

"My pleasure." It sounded like he meant it, but his eyes were guarded.

Clearly, she wasn't the only one still aching from their talk Saturday night.

Wynn tapped the side of his boot against Liam's. "Clemmie says you're leaving to work far away."

Liam ruffled Wynn's hair. "A little earlier than planned, yeah."

"Clemmie showed us where you're going on the globe. It's a long way from here, just like Grammy and Grampy in Uganda." Annie's eyes narrowed. "When will you be back?"

"I'm not sure, but I'll visit Widow's Peak Creek more often than I have in the past."

Considering it had been years since he last dropped by, that could mean anything.

Clementine's stomach ached. She'd known both kids had grown fond of Liam, but they'd become more attached than she'd expected. Wanting him as their uncle? They must be so hurt right now. Had she made a huge mistake, allowing Liam in her life again so she could gain closure, when it had caused the kids pain?

There was always a price to be paid, wasn't there? If closure couldn't have been gained without the kids getting hurt, she wished she'd left it alone. This wasn't what she'd wanted at all.

At least You've given me the opportunity to shut the door on my past with Liam for good, and for that, I thank You, God. I wish I didn't still feel drawn to him. I wish the kids weren't so fond of him. Help me to trust You as we move forward from here.

Wynn stayed fixed to Liam's side as they gathered on the porch and Liam unpacked his equipment. Liam showed the kids the white drone, then the controller with two joysticks and a touchscreen. He glanced up at her. "I thought we'd start filming at the berry patch and send the drone northward over the sheep to the creek. The battery only lasts about twenty minutes, so when it needs a charge, I can film close-ups of the sheep with a different camera."

"Perfect. I'll try to stay out of your way."

"You're not watching with us?"

Her throat clogged with emotion. "I wish I could, but Eleanor is missing again."

"What do you mean, missing?"

"She was in the field an hour ago. Then I found a wasp nest on one of the roof's wings and had to get the ladder out." It hadn't been easy, climbing even halfway up that ladder without hyperventilating, but she'd done it. "I don't know if Eleanor disappeared while I was in the barn or on the roof, because by the time I got down from the ladder, I looked back at the field, and she was gone."

"Eleanor's the one who was on Fergus's property last month, right?"

"Yes, so she's had a taste of freedom." That didn't bode well, but she couldn't think about that right now.

She had to search for a breach in the fence to indicate where Eleanor could've gone. But honestly, they'd been checked more in the past six weeks than they had all year. How had she missed yet another tear?

"Mr. Campbell's gonna yell if he finds Eleanor eating his grass," Annie said.

"Let's hope not." Clementine forced a smile. "I wish I had his phone number so I could ask if he sees her on his land, but he's refused to share with me. Anyway, I'd better look for the hole."

Liam set down the controls. "I'll help, and we'll cover the ground twice as fast."

"No need. You guys can go ahead with the drone, if you don't mind me running off for a minute. The doctor wants Annie to take it easy for a few days—"

"I'll see to it, Clementine."

High-pitched *mehs* carried from the field. Eleanor's lambs must have figured out she wasn't nearby. *Help me find her, Lord.*

"I'm praying, too." Liam's touch on her elbow was no more than a graze, but she felt the nerves all the way to her shoulder.

"Thanks." She hurried away, rubbing her arm where the gentle pressure of his touch still lingered. She'd found permanent closure on her relationship with Liam, all right. They lived two different lives.

But that didn't mean her heart got the message. She could only pray God would ultimately heal her of her feelings for Liam Murphy, and that his leaving wouldn't break her kids' hearts, too.

Watching Clementine rush into the field with the sheep, Liam tamped down his frustration. He wanted to help search for wayward Eleanor. Wanted to comfort Clementine. How must she be feeling now, with her fences tearing over and over like this? All these rips and holes seemed statistically unlikely, considering what good care Clementine took of her farm. No, the damage had to be deliberate.

Unless Fergus Campbell had been right when he said she was missing things. Liam didn't believe that, though. Something was off, and it wasn't Clementine's farm management.

A pat on his shoulder drew his attention back to the kids. Wynn's eyes crinkled at the corners. "Is the drone okay?"

"Fine. We have to set up." He explained the process in terms they could understand, leaving out all the technical stuff. Then he showed them the controller. "You must not touch this, but you can watch the screen here to see what the drone captures on film."

"Wynn and I can't fly it around?" Annie's lower lip protruded.

"I'm sorry, but no. I had to get a special license to fly the drone." He narrated his actions and answered their questions about what random buttons did, and he was about to get the drone airborne when Clementine jogged back across the field, her brows pulled low.

He stood up. "No success?"

"No Eleanor, but I found a wedge big enough for her to get through to Fergus's place," she called as she let herself out the gate. "Inches away from the zip ties you helped me with when you first got here."

Liam met her on the driveway. "How is that possible? We were thorough."

"I'm positive this rip isn't an accident. The cuts are

clean." Her eyes sparked fire. "I don't know what I'm going to do about it—I'll patch it tonight and maybe go buy a motion sensor camera. Right now, though, I'd better go knock on Fergus's door. I need to get Eleanor back. You don't mind being alone with the kids a little longer?"

"Not at all." Although he wished he could go with her to be there if that crank next door got salty with her. *She doesn't need you, though. Never did, never will.*

The best way Liam could help her was to attend to the kids.

She jogged to the barn, and when she emerged seconds later with a length of cord, he was about to launch the drone. "Behave for Mr. Liam, guys. No running around, Annie."

"Okay," Annie shouted before patting Liam's arm. "Do you think Clemmie will have to sell her?"

"Who, Eleanor?"

Wynn's nod was far too mature-looking for his years. "She's escaped more than once now. It means she's got a taste for adventure, and that's not good in a sheep."

Liam could hear Clementine in every word of that sentence. And if he'd forgotten that a "taste for adventure" wasn't a good thing in this house, a glance at Annie's cast was a solid reminder.

But now that he thought about it, he could see that adventure wasn't good for a sheep. A wandering ewe could lead her lambs and others astray, and the world was full of dangers. As a bad example, Eleanor couldn't be allowed to stay here, could she?

Liam refused to think about the parallels between himself and a sheep who had a hankering to explore.

Not right now anyway, not with two kids whose fretful expressions grew more serious by the second.

How to reassure them? He couldn't tell them everything would turn out okay, because he didn't want to mislead them. But he couldn't just leave them worried, either. "Tell you what, let's wait and see what happened with Eleanor before we wonder what's going to happen. In fact, we ought to pray about it."

Wynn offered him a hand to hold and Annie snuggled into Liam's side. His heart about split in half. These were the most precious kids on earth. *Lord, help me here. I don't want them hurt.*

His prayer wouldn't win any eloquence awards, but the words came from his heart as he thanked God for Eleanor and asked God to keep watch over her. For the fences to hold until the new one Clemmie bought could be installed. For the kids.

Their loud "amens" accompanied a hard squeeze to his fingers from Wynn. Three squeezes, in fact. Back in the day, when Liam and Clementine held hands, on occasion she'd give his hand three squeezes. Each squeeze held a message.

I-love-you. One word per squeeze. She'd passed her code on to her children, while he'd forgotten it altogether. Had it really been that long since he had loved anyone enough to squeeze their hands and share a secret code like that?

"I feel better," Annie said.

Wynn nodded. "Me, too."

"Why don't we get the drone in the air, then, so we have some great footage to show your aunt when she gets back."

Once the drone was airborne, the kids *oohed* with

excitement. Martha barked at it as it made its whirring ascent off the driveway, but its noise was soon eclipsed by the sputtering hum of some sort of large vehicle like a tractor somewhere in the neighborhood. Thankfully, the noise didn't affect Liam's footage, but it might affect how successful Clementine was at talking to Fergus, especially if he was the one using the farm equipment.

"Look, it's the berry patch." Annie's voice was excited as she stared at the screen.

"And Dolley." The volume of Wynn's voice rose with each syllable.

Dolley glanced up at the drone but didn't bark. Aware as she was of the thing flying over her, she remained calm, collected. Surely she'd noted Eleanor wandering off, but whatever had happened when the ewe disappeared hadn't caused the Great Pyrenees much in the way of concern or angst.

Lord, help me focus on the task at hand while You help Clementine. I don't want the kids to worry, and I want to give Clementine this one last gift of footage for her website.

In a moment of great timing, one of the lambs leaped and kicked in a storybook-perfect display of joy. That was gold-star video for the website—

Gold star. Like the name of the festival recipe contest. He might be leaving Widow's Peak Creek in the morning, but the memories of this extended stay would rise at unexpected times in the coming weeks, wouldn't it? He'd never really break free.

The kids' running commentary drew him back to the present. He had to admit, the footage was looking good. Great lighting showed off the farm in its springtime glory, manifest in bright green grass, blooming flowers in the garden and lush leaves on the trees.

Those trees by the creek, however? A bit of an unforeseen problem.

"Why is the drone coming back this way?" Wynn looked up from the screen. "I thought you were going to film the creek."

"That was my plan, but the trees are denser than I thought, so I have to bring the drone back, lower the altitude and go back in to capture the creek."

Annie started to lose interest as he navigated the drone. He caught her fitfulness from the corner of his eye, and though she tried to be slow and sneaky, he couldn't miss her inching down the porch steps. "Annie, where are you going?"

"I want to swing."

Still piloting the drone, he glanced up for a nanosecond. "Your aunt said no running around, with your broken arm."

"It's not running. And I don't need two arms to hold on to the swing."

"I hear you, but it's best you stay here with me until Clemmie comes back. Look, I'm sending the drone down low to film the creek. Do you think we'll see a fish?"

"There aren't fish in there. Pleases can I swing?"

Sara's white sedan pulled into the driveway, adding another element to the numerous things pulling at his attention. What was she doing here? And how did parents ever get anything done with so many distractions? "Annie, I told Clemmie you'd stay here with me until she comes back. Come all the way back onto the porch while the car's coming, please."

Sara parked in front of the house. Liam waved at her, but he was sure his expression looked confused rather than happy about her arrival.

"What's that?" Wynn's pat on Liam's arm was almost frantic.

Liam's head swiveled back to the screen. "What did you see?"

"A fish?" Annie's loud voice sounded incredulous.

"No. It was a big blue purse. Clemmie doesn't have a blue purse." Wynn pointed to the left of the screen, like Liam needed to guide the drone that direction again.

"Maybe you saw a rock." There'd been a few small gray boulders on the north side of the creek.

"A rock isn't blue." Wynn sounded offended.

"You're right, buddy. Just wondering if the light's giving a rock a bluish tint."

"Hey, guys." Sara strolled toward the porch. "How's the filming?"

"I saw a purse." Wynn's arms folded.

"That's a weird thing to find." Sara's wedge boots thunked on the porch steps.

It would be an odd discovery indeed, but Liam couldn't fathom how a purse that didn't belong to Clementine would end up by the creek. Maybe kids had come over the fence again but leaving a large purse behind didn't seem likely. Wynn must have seen something else. There was only one way to put the matter to rest, though.

"In a minute I'll go back that way to look for the purse." He scanned the screen, glancing up at his sister. "Sara, what brings you here?"

"I thought I'd talk to Clementine."

About what? Her and their mom's roles in his and Clementine's breakup a zillion years ago? Yesterday, he'd wanted to talk to Sara about it as well as how he could support her in her marriage, but when he and Grandma came home after church, she'd been on the phone with Dane. He'd spent the rest of his day tying up loose ends and saying his goodbyes, having dinner with Kellan and Paige, and today, he'd met Benton and Joel for lunch.

But he should tell Sara he wanted to talk. "When the filming's over, you and I need to—"

"Need to what?" Sara looked over his shoulder.

"Wynn's right. There's a blue bag. I think it's a backpack." Liam zoomed the camera, his muscles tensing so hard he might break his equipment if he wasn't careful.

To his shock, two feet away from the backpack was another surprise. Fergus Campbell, kneeling beside Blue Creek, a round, shallow pan in hand.

"Mr. Campbell's panning for gold." Wynn grabbed Liam's arm.

"You have gold on your farm? Cool." Sara sat on the porch swing.

"Not cool when the neighbor is stealing it. And took a sheep to divert our attention." Liam piloted the drone to hover over Eleanor. Tied to a tree with a rope looped through her collar, the ewe munched on the greenery underfoot. She seemed okay, but if she wasn't in perfect condition when this was over…?

Liam's vision darkened. "Sara, keep the kids with you on the porch and call the cops."

"You're serious? He's stealing Clementine's stuff? What are you doing?"

"Recalling the drone to home base." He turned to the kids and put a hand on each of their shoulders. "Stay here on the porch with Sara. Do not touch the controls.

The drone will come back all by itself. I'm going to talk to Fergus."

"Shouldn't we wait for the police?" Sara asked in a stage whisper as if that meant the kids couldn't hear her.

"I don't want him getting away. Clearly, the neighbor's equipment drowned out the noise of the drone, so he has no idea we've got him on film." He leaped down the porch steps. "Clemmie should be back any second."

"Mr. Liam?" Annie's eyes welled with tears.

"It's okay. Sara's got you. It'll all be okay, I promise."

He might not be around to see these kids grow up, but the least he could do was keep his promises to them.

Chapter Fifteen

Liam shoved his way through the last gate to the northern paddock and burst into the trees at the creek's edge, fists clenched. But only Eleanor was there, chewing, eyeing him with disinterest. Liam thanked God she wasn't hurt, but Fergus was not where Liam had seen him on the touchscreen. Had the gold-thieving liar heard the drone, or—

A loud splash drew Liam westward into the trees, toward the ponding basin.

Fergus floundered in the water beyond the reeds lining the edge, clearly unable to swim.

"Fergus!" Liam sprinted to the water's border. "Can you touch bottom?" Then he remembered something about the pond having been dredged. Was it too deep to stand in? How on earth had he fallen into the basin anyway?

"Help," Fergus got out between splutters of water.

If only he'd brought a rope or a phone or something. All Liam had was himself.

No, that wasn't true. He had the Lord.

Praying, he crouched on the muddy edge and reached

out, just missing Fergus's fingertips. "Kick, Fergus. Kick your legs over this way."

Fergus's head dipped below the murky surface. Fast as he could, Liam unlaced his boots, stripped out of his socks and jumped into the pond.

The water was ice-cold, jarring him to the bone. He spat out a foul-tasting mouthful of water and swam to where Fergus floundered. Scooping beneath the man's armpit to clamp him about the torso, Liam struggled to swim back toward the reeds. Fergus flailed from his grip, and Liam tried again. "Stay with me, Fergus. Stop thrashing."

Fergus twisted and the back of his hard skull smacked the left side of Liam's chest. Pain speared his collarbone. He must have cried out, because Fergus went still. Or at least, his upper half did. His legs were all over the place. Was he kicking to help out?

Clenching his teeth against the pain radiating from his collarbone, Liam scissors-kicked and hauled Fergus back to the reeds. *God, God*—it was all he could pray. No words formed among the blinding pain setting off signals in his brain.

His foot touched the slimy bottom, almost slipped out from under him, but he regained his balance. "It's shallow here. Grab hold of the reeds and pull yourself out." Liam demonstrated, pulling himself up on muddy ground with his arms.

Wheezing, Fergus grabbed, but his hands slid from the reeds. He tried again but panted, too tired to haul himself up alongside Liam. Unable to find purchase with his feet. Unable to get out.

Liam rolled to his stomach, arms outstretched. "Grab my wrists."

Clasped at the wrist, Liam tugged, got his knees under him for leverage, and tugged harder. Fergus slid out, deadweight, and smacked into Liam's chest, knocking him onto his back.

Liam didn't feel the load. All he could feel was his collarbone. It might have re-broken, for the pain it caused.

Fergus rolled away, gasping for breath.

Once Liam could speak around the agony in his left shoulder, he stared at Fergus. "Stealing gold I understand, but why on earth did you get into that pond?"

"You know…about the gold?" The words came between pants.

"I saw you panning through my drone camera. All the fencing accidents, the lies about kids hopping fences? It was you, because you found gold over here. But why'd you get in the pond if you can't swim?"

"Why'd you save me if you knew what I'd done?"

Mud-soaked, dripping wet, Liam stood and extended a hand to Fergus. Fergus accepted, and though it sent fresh spears of pain through his core, Liam pulled him up. "Not sure what kind of man you take me for, Fergus Campbell."

"My glasses. My pan." Fergus looked longingly at the pond.

"I think those are the least of your worries." Liam tramped off to get his shoes, breathing through the pain piercing his collarbone. Clementine would be so relieved Eleanor was safe. Much as he hated that Fergus had done so much to make Clementine's life miserable, at least now they had answers. Fergus's behavior explained everything.

His relief fled when the neighbor's farming equipment fell silent, and the sound was replaced by a child's scream.

Liam left his shoes behind and, ignoring the agony he felt, ran, begging God for help.

Clementine heard the child's piercing cry all the way from the road. She ran so hard back to the farm her side hurt, but pain was the last thing on her mind when she raced up the driveway and saw Wynn, half up on the barn roof, his legs dangling down.

Nausea roiled through her. She fought against the familiar sensations wrought by panic—the prickling skin, the inability to breathe, the overwhelming sense of doom—and ran on shaky legs. She mustn't scream, even though she wanted to. She mustn't frighten Wynn. One false move, and he could slip off the barn.

The thought increased her nausea and doubled her pace.

Where was Annie? *Oh, thank You, Lord.* Sara held Annie on her hip while holding a phone to her ear. Where was Liam? Up on the roof? Did he go up there, leaving Wynn to follow? Anger tinged her anxiety.

Explanations could wait, though. Clementine rushed to stand beneath Wynn, jumping over the ladder lying flat on the ground. It must've fallen after Wynn climbed up. If he'd been on the ladder when it fell? Clementine forced the frightening thought from her mind and held up her arms as if they could stretch to him. "Wynn, I'm here, baby."

"Clemmie." His voice was so small.

"Hold on. Is Liam up there to pull you?"

"No, he's not, Clementine," Sara yelled at her, holding the phone away from her mouth. Then she returned the phone, rattling off Clementine's address. "Send the fire department as well as the police. Please, hurry."

The police? What was going on?

Meanwhile, Wynn was going to fall before her eyes. *Lord, help us.* She lifted the ladder from the ground, wrestling its weight until it leaned against the barn wall below Wynn's feet. Before she had it squared, however, her nephew hauled himself up with his arms, threw a leg up and scrambled up on the roof. Her pounding heart about exploded out of her chest.

It didn't help when his tears-bright eyes peeked over the edge of the roof. "Clemmie?"

"Don't move, okay?"

A shout drew her gaze around. Liam ran toward her from the north end of the property, his left arm tight to his chest as if it were still in a sling. Several yards behind him, a denim-clad guy followed at a slower pace. Fergus. That explained why Fergus hadn't answered his front door to her repeated rings of the bell, but what was he doing on Honeysuckle Farm?

And why did they look…wet? Had they been in her pond?

Liam came straight for her, his eyes wide. "What's happening?"

"I don't know." Clementine tried to breathe, but her lungs felt squeezed, like she'd been underwater too long. "Annie, are you okay?"

"Wynn dropped the controller and broke it," Annie said through tears.

"I'm so sorry, Liam." Sara held the phone away from her agony-stricken face. "It's my fault. The drone ended up crashing on the roof."

Liam was paler than she'd ever seen him. "It couldn't have crashed. I set it on return to base."

Sara's eyes filled with tears. "I called 9-1-1, and next thing I know, Wynn is climbing the ladder, and Annie said the drone crashed, and then you came, Clementine. I blew it, just like I always knew I would. I'm so sorry."

Clementine was the one who'd left the ladder out. She had no idea what was happening that required police or why Liam and Fergus were wet, or why Fergus was even here. "No one could have predicted this, Sara." Whatever *this* was. "Thanks for keeping Annie safe and calling 9-1-1. I can't wait for the police to arrive to get Wynn down, though." His crying set her anxiety on overdrive.

"I'm going after him." Liam grabbed hold of the ladder with his right hand.

Relief tinged the rough edges of her panic. "Thank you, Liam. I don't want him alone." But when Liam adjusted the ladder, his grimace indicated he was in great discomfort, and his pallor was practically bloodless. Something must've happened to reinjure his collarbone. That was why he kept his left arm so close to his body, and oh, she didn't like how he was blinking, like he was seeing stars.

"Liam?"

"I'm fine." But his lips spread in an anguished wince.

"Stubborn mule." Fergus joined them, hurrying to grip the ladder beneath Liam. "You're gonna black out from pain, and then we'll need two ambulances. I'll go to the boy."

Liam's head turned down. "Not sure your knees can handle this, Fergus."

Fergus looked different without his glasses on. His

eyes were smaller, more frightened, but that stomp of his foot proved he was determined to be taken seriously. "I'll make 'em handle it. None of this would've happened if it weren't for me."

What did that mean? Clementine wanted to cry along with Wynn, but she held back. Answers would come once Wynn was on the ground.

Liam half slipped off the ladder climbing down to exchange places with Fergus. Her gaze dropped to his left collarbone and held back a gasp. She hadn't realized before, but the area was swollen.

She wished she could do something for Liam, but Wynn's cries broke Clementine's heart as Fergus mounted the ladder and made a painfully slow ascent up three rungs. "Nope. These ol' knees aren't gonna do it. Just wait for the fire department."

Shouldn't she hear sirens by now? Panic ate away at her, clouded her thoughts, made her want to curl on the ground.

What did Benton tell her, last time they talked about her panic attacks in his office at the church? Something about pinpointing her brain on something true, like a piece of Scripture. Focusing. Considering the meaning of God's word.

The Lord is my Shepherd...

What did that even mean, that God was a shepherd? It was so hard to focus with Wynn crying up on the roof. Her panic wouldn't help him, though. She needed to get control so she could be of use to her children.

The Lord is my Shepherd...

She was a shepherd, so she should understand this Psalm, right? A shepherd showed compassion. Provision. Delight in his or her sheep.

And tough love.

Why did that pop into her mind? But there it was. Not images of sweet moments with the sheep, the gentle scratches atop the head, the baby talk and cooing, the joy of watching the lambs frolic over the grass. Those things were precious and important, yes, but they were not the same as *tough love*.

Tough love was doing what was best for the sheep, not the things she, or they, enjoyed. Enforcing boundaries so they didn't wander into trouble. Ensuring cleanliness. Providing for their physical needs. Proving herself a faithful presence.

No way was she comparing her care for her little flock to the love and provision of Jesus, the True Shepherd, but she could see some small-scale parallels. God could see more than she could, a bigger picture, and His hand was active. Not just in her life, but the kids' lives, too. He could be trusted.

The kids had lost so much already, though. What if Wynn fell and—

No, enough of that. The sheep trusted Clementine. It was time she entrusted her life to the Shepherd.

She mounted the ladder.

I trust You. Help me trust You more—

Clementine had gone up two rungs before Liam reached her. "You're afraid of heights. I'll try again, Clem, with all I have in me. I'll get to him."

Liam's ragged breath told her how much pain he was in, though. So did the flat jet of his eyes. Poor Liam. "I know you would. But it's my turn."

She didn't know how she'd make it, but she wouldn't let Wynn be alone up there.

And what had Liam told Wynn? "When your nerves get the best of you, remember God is with you." All right, she was remembering.

I'm scared, God. But You know that already. Ankles wobbling, she climbed another rung. *You are my Shepherd.*

"Doing great, Clementine!"

Liam's voice lightened her emotional load a fraction. She was almost to the top now. One more rung and her line of vision reached the rooftop. Her gaze locked on to Wynn's wide-eyed stare.

"Clemmie." Fresh tears started as he inched closer.

"Stay right there, baby. I'm coming to you." With a prayer, she boosted herself onto the roof. As she scooted her knees beneath her and crawled toward Wynn, the hot roof tiles scraped her palms, but the security of something beneath her felt wonderful.

"Got him," she hollered over her shoulder to those below.

Liam yelled something back that she couldn't make out, but his tone was relieved.

Oh, the sound of sirens was a wonderful thing. She crept back farther from the edge, sat cross-legged and pulled Wynn onto her lap.

Wynn settled deeper into her embrace. "We aren't going down?"

"Help's coming, and we'll go down with them." She'd trusted God to get her up here, but the brain He'd given her told her the fire department would do a better job ensuring their safe descent than she could manage. "For now, let's enjoy the view."

"I'm sorry, Clemmie. Liam told me not to touch the controller, but the battery was getting low, so I thought

I should help. Then I dropped it and the antennae broke, and the drone crashed on the barn. Miss Sara and Annie didn't even notice because of Fergus panning for gold in our creek, and I thought maybe if I hurried real fast and got the drone down, no one would know what I did." He started to cry again. "You told me not to get on the ladder, too. You're mad at me."

"I'm not mad, sweetheart." She wiped tears from his cheeks. "I'm just glad you're safe. What's this about Fergus panning for gold in Blue Creek?"

"Clemmie, it was something." His voice calmed as he moved into story mode. His tale of the drone capturing a blue purse that looked like a diaper bag and Mr. Liam getting so mad his hands fisted had her riveted. As he talked, a bright red fire engine and a black-and-white police car pulled into the driveway.

There was a lot awaiting her down on the ground, but for the moment, she took the time to be grateful. She laid her cheek atop Wynn's head.

Thank You, Shepherd.

Chapter Sixteen

The moment Clementine's feet touched solid ground, she was caught in a bear hug that encompassed her and both kids, gripped so tight she could hardly breathe. But the breaths she took were tinged with cedarwood, and the chest beneath her cheek was solid. Liam. She shut her eyes.

"You're safe now." Liam's voice was soft in her ear. "I'm so sorry—"

"I'm so sorry," she said at the exact moment.

His head pulled back. "You have nothing to be sorry about, Clementine, but I've got a hundred and one."

"I'm hot." Annie wriggled out of the group hug.

Clementine eased back, too, but Wynn leaned into Liam, bursting into tears again. "I'm sorry I broke your drone and the controller."

"Those things can be fixed or replaced, but there's no replacing you, buddy. Which reminds me, does anything hurt?"

Wynn swiped his eyes. "I'm good."

"Me, too," Clementine said. Physically, anyway. "But

you, Liam Murphy, need a doctor. Your collarbone area looks really swollen."

"I'll be all right." Liam's smile had a white ring around it, though, indicating he was in pain, heaps of it. What had happened to reinjure it?

"Ma'am?" One of the police officers beckoned her over.

Oh yeah. Fergus.

Her neighbor wiped his hair with one of her beach towels, and Sara offered another to Liam. Annie must have told her they were kept in the hall cupboard. Clementine accompanied the young, blond police officer to join his black-haired partner and Fergus, pausing to thank and hug the firefighters along the way.

Everyone smiled except for Fergus, who wrapped the beach towel around him like a shawl.

"You all right, Fergus?"

His small eyes squinted at her. "That don't matter. How are you and the boy?"

Her hands extended. "No worse for the experience, but I'm not sure I can say the same for you and Liam. What happened?"

"Ma'am," the police officer answered instead of Fergus. "Mr. Campbell states he was trespassing, but that might be the least of charges filed against him."

"I'd like to speak to him alone, please."

"Ma'am?"

"Just for a minute." She caught Liam's questioning gaze and beckoned him over. She'd like his take, too, since he'd been the one to confront Fergus, but the kids didn't need to be in on this. "Sara, would you mind helping the kids get popsicles from the freezer?"

"On it. C'mon, guys. What flavors do you have?"

The slam of the screen door told her when the kids were out of earshot, so she turned her gaze to Fergus. "Is Eleanor safe?"

"Fine as frog hair, still tied to a tree on the other side of the creek. I'm sorry for taking her like that. I wasn't going to keep her, just hold her long enough so you'd be busy looking for her and fixing fences. I had to hurry and pan what I could before you put in that electric fencing and I couldn't get in."

She'd hardly been able to believe it when, on the roof, Wynn told her Fergus was panning for gold in her creek. "I had no idea there was gold."

"People think all the gold in Widow's Peak Creek was gone a long time ago, but there's still a bit, and it's flowing into your tributary."

"It can't be worth that much, though." Liam cradled his left arm against his chest.

"It ain't. But the first time I met you, missy, your little girl showed me the red rocks in her pocket. Found them at her creek, she said. Red rocks can be iron-rich, and iron sometimes goes hand in hand with gold. All those big rocks you got there are quartz. Same thing."

"Quartz is white, isn't it?"

"Iron staining makes it look dirty. Not always a clue, but worth investigating. I can't prove it, but I'm sure you've got a vein beneath the spot where Blue Creek flows into the ponding basin. The vein must've gotten nicked when the basin was dug deeper, since you said it happened in the past few years. You'll have to dig for it to get a significant amount, of course."

"That's why you wanted to buy my property." To use the necessary equipment to get the gold.

"You didn't know what you had. No one ever knows

what they have." Fergus swiped his damp face. Were the drops trickling down his cheeks from his still-wet hair, or were they tears? "I didn't used to be like this. Or maybe I was, and that's why my wife had enough of me. The only thing I know how to do is drive everyone away."

Oh boy. There was a story and a half here, and Clementine's heart pinched. She still had questions, though. "Did you damage my fence?"

When Fergus choked back a sob, Liam shifted on his feet. "I have a theory. Fergus messed with the fence in several places to throw off suspicion. If he'd only damaged the fence in areas where he could reach Blue Creek, we'd have figured out what he was up to a lot sooner. Instead, he created distraction after distraction. The berry patch, the story about the kids trespassing, saying Eleanor was on his land—there were never any kids, and I doubt Eleanor ever slipped into his property. Fergus just made it look like you couldn't properly care for your fences, planting seeds of doubt in your head so you'd sell to him."

Fergus wiped his nose with the back of his hand. "That about sums it up. I've got a black heart."

"I don't think so. You could've run away when we heard Wynn's cry from the pond," Liam said gently. "But you didn't. You even tried to help, taking to the ladder despite your bad knees."

Liam was right. Despite all the damage Fergus had done to her property, he was coming clean now. "I appreciate you telling the truth."

"I don't deserve a lick of appreciation, missy, but this here fellow does. When I was digging at the edge of your pond, my knees gave out and I fell in. I should've been a goner, but he saved me. Even though he already knew

I was a thief and a liar. You know it, too, but you're giving me towels and kindness. You and those young'uns deserve better than what I did to you. I'm sorry, missy."

"I forgive you."

"Might be all words, but it's more than I deserve."

"No, I mean it." Clementine reached to touch his bony shoulder. "I didn't do anything to deserve God's mercy. That's why we're supposed to extend it to each other, too." Clementine glanced at Liam. There was so much between them that remained unresolved. So many wounds. They might not be meant to be together, but she'd never really let him go, despite her best intentions.

She would now. She cared for him, so she had to set him—and her sorrow over their past—free, into God's hands.

Liam's gaze met hers with such fierceness, she couldn't help but wonder if he was thinking the same thing.

Fergus dug into his pocket and pulled out a soiled baggie of water-filled glass tubes. "This is what I found today, and there's more at my house. Not a lot of money's worth but it's yours. And if I get out of jail on bail and you can stomach the sight of me, I'll help you fix everything I damaged. I'll even help install that fancy new fence you say is coming in."

"Oh, Fergus." She knew so little about him, other than that he had chickens and was cranky. And that he was utterly alone.

Taking the baggie, she realized how rich she was. Not in gold, but in so much more.

"Officers?" Clementine stepped toward them. "Thank you so much for everything, but I don't wish to press charges."

* * *

"Ready to head over to the emergency room, Liam?" Sara looked up from her spot in the wicker porch chair where she'd bent down to rub Martha's head. The golden retriever's thick tail wagged in low sweeps over the porch.

"I suppose so." There was no use procrastinating any longer. He'd done all he could here at Honeysuckle Farm, thanking the first responders with Clementine before they all walked to the creek. They retrieved Eleanor and searched for Fergus's glasses, which Sara discovered in the mud by a cluster of reeds, while Annie pointed out every red-brown rock she could find to Wynn, so they could check for gold specks. After that, Clementine sent Fergus home with the request that he come over for lunch the following day to talk to her and Rex about installing the new fencing.

Liam would love to know how that lunch went, but he'd be halfway to Los Angeles by noon tomorrow—if the ER doc gave the go-ahead, that is. Liam's pain was lessening, though, and surely that wouldn't be the case if his collarbone had broken again.

Besides, Grandma would give him the scoop on the outcome of Clementine and Fergus's discussion anyway. It was all in God's hands.

The sun dipped low, turning the sky a deeper shade of azure. The kids would be hungry for dinner soon, and then the sheep would need milking. It was time to get out of Clementine's hair.

Forever, this time. Because tomorrow he was leaving, and even though he might visit, it would never be the same.

He finished packing up his busted equipment while

Clementine chatted on the driveway with an older neighbor couple who'd seen the emergency vehicles. The kids didn't seem any worse for wear after this afternoon's ordeal, sitting in the field near the sheep. Liam took a mental film of the adorable scene.

"Want to know something funny?" Sara stood up. "The reason I came here today was to apologize to you and Clementine for something. Remember back when you were seventeen?"

"Is this about you and Mom encouraging her to break up with me?"

She gaped. "You knew about that? Wow, yes, that was what I was going to tell you. Mom and I thought it best, seeing as you two were so different, but we shouldn't have interfered. You must hate me. Both of you must hate me, Clementine especially. I mean, I can't babysit worth beans. I shouldn't be a mom after all."

"After all? Did you change your mind about having a family?" This was a big conversation they could never finish here on Clementine's porch, but he couldn't drop the subject unacknowledged.

"The truth is, I've always wanted a kid. Three, actually. But I've been so afraid of being a bad mom, I pushed down that part of myself. Then this last Saturday, seeing all the kids and their pets, I couldn't deny it to myself any longer. I do want a family."

"But after what happened today, you're waffling again?"

"I did, for a half hour or so, because I made a mistake, but I've learned something from watching Clementine. She didn't yell at me, she forgave Fergus, and through her panic and everything, she kept going. Life is a roller coaster, with parts that make you laugh and other parts that make you sick to your stomach, but she's buckled in for the ride, isn't she?"

"She is." And despite her panic, she'd faced her fears to get to Wynn. She was as brave as she was beautiful.

"She does *not* have her act together. At all. But she has God and gumption, and those get her through. I want that, too. God and gumption."

"You have plenty of gumption, sis. We can talk about the God part."

"Okay." She gave him a watery smile. "I've noticed a difference in you since you decided to follow God, and I want to be different, too." She sighed. "I'll stay one more day with Grandma, and then I'll head home to work things out with Dane."

"I'm glad. Your marriage is definitely worth fighting for." Liam gave Martha a goodbye rubdown. The sweet golden retriever thumped her tail.

"I'd thought real love meant there wouldn't ever be complications. No disagreements, no being out of step. I was wrong." Sara stood. "Love is worth it, though."

At that moment, Clementine waved goodbye to the neighbors and moved back to the porch. Her gaze met Liam's and held.

"Do you understand what I'm saying, Liam?" Sara's hissed whisper wasn't subtle. "Love is worth fighting for."

"Yeah, you and Dane are going to work at things."

"You're such a dummy." Sara grabbed her purse from behind a wicker chair and clomped down the porch steps.

He wasn't that big of a dummy. But Sara was married. He was not. There was nothing to fight for here but further heartache. Certainly not love.

Sara hugged Clementine. "I'd better get this knucklehead to the emergency room, Clementine."

Clementine frowned at his collarbone. "I hope it's not broken again."

"I don't think it is. Aggravated, yes, but it shouldn't hamper my trip to Indonesia."

"That's great." Clementine sounded as if she meant it.

Perhaps she, like him, was ready to start fresh. It was time for life to return to normal.

Liam carried the larger case down the porch steps. Clementine ran for the smaller case and helped him pack the trunk. She didn't look at him at all but turned her head toward the pasture. "Kids, Liam's leaving now. Come say goodbye."

As they came toward the fence, Liam once again took in the scene so he could look back on the memory later. The grazing sheep. Fluffy Martha. The cottonwoods, flowers and berry bushes, and the peaks of the Sierra Nevada looming beyond. Wynn, ruddy cheeked, and Annie, her pink cast as bright as her smile.

Liam opened the gate for them so they could meet him on the driveway.

Wynn reached in for a hug, but Annie stood back. "When are you coming back?"

"I don't know."

"What about Christmas?"

"Maybe, but I might be with my mom." It had been a long time since they'd seen one another, and he should reach out. "I'll send postcards from Indonesia, though. I've heard there are beaches with pink sand."

"I love pink," Annie announced, to no one's surprise.

Wynn reached for Liam's hand and squeezed three times. *I-love-you.*

Oh boy. How could he leave like this? But he had to. Yet another reason he'd never forged ties. Leaving was too hard when it went hand in hand with difficult goodbyes.

"Love you, too," he said around the lump in his throat.

"My turn to tell you munchkins goodbye." Sara extended her arms for hugs. "I almost forgot. Will you show me Bo Peep's mom before we go?"

The kids led her down the fence line to find Lady Bird, and Liam was grateful for his sister's blatant ploy to give him a minute with Clementine. He swallowed down the lump in a painful gulp.

"I'm not sure I got enough footage for your website, but I'll send you what there is. Sorry I didn't get more photos of the ewes for their bios."

"I still have to write them up anyway. Thanks for doing all of that for me." Clementine bit her lip, a sign she was feeling more than she wanted to let on.

That made two of them, but there was no use dragging this out. Still, he had one last thing to say.

"I'm sorry."

"You have nothing to be sorry for. You figured out what Fergus was up to and you tried to get to Wynn. You're a superhero."

Hardly. He'd never experienced fear like he had when Clementine and Wynn were up on the roof. He better understood Clementine's anxiety now, because he was more scared of something bad happening to her and the kids than he'd been climbing Mount Everest. How backward was he, that he was thirty-three years old and just now felt scared over losing someone?

Maybe if he'd understood this sort of thing sooner he wouldn't be such a lost cause. But it was too late now.

"I'm glad we found our way to being friends again. It's more than I hoped for when I came back to Widow's Peak Creek."

"Me, too." She forced a smile. "Stay safe out there, okay? No more broken bones if you can help it."

"And you keep on trusting God. You did great today."

Even though it hurt.

"Goodbye, Liam."

"Goodbye, Clementine."

The words were final, but he was all smiles and waves while the kids could see him. *Take care of them, Lord.*

God hadn't quite answered his prayer for complete closure, not the way his heart felt as if it splintered in his chest while he drove away from Honeysuckle Farm, tailing Sara in her car.

But he was a better man for having been around Clementine these past five weeks. And he was learning sometimes a wound was a good thing when it came to keeping a body close to God.

And God would use the pain for a purpose in Liam's life. Somehow.

Chapter Seventeen

Clementine fanned her hot cheeks with her hand. The calendar might say mid-May, but the weather seemed to think they'd jumped straight into July. Not even noon yet, and already Widow's Peak Creek was sweltering hot. She was sticky, sweaty and in need of a full glass of water.

It didn't help that her house was filling up. The other members of the Gold Rush Days committee were all arriving for their wrap-up meeting to evaluate how the festival had gone. Clementine didn't have air-conditioning, and the others probably wished they'd chosen to meet somewhere else.

Everyone had arrived except for Faith, but already, the other committee members had made quick work of the pitchers of cold drinks she'd set out. The iced tea was still half full, but the water pitcher was already empty except for an ice cube and the slices of cucumber she'd added for flavor. Clementine scooped up the pitcher with a smile. "I'll be back with a refill."

When the kids came home from school, they'd go wade in the creek. And who knows, maybe they'd find a flake or two of gold.

"That's a sight for sore eyes."

Clementine hadn't heard Marigold follow her from the family room. While not a member of the committee, Marigold had driven Trudie and Eileen over from the retirement village. Clementine invited her to stay, saying the winner of the Gold Star Favorite recipe contest could sit in on their wrap-up meeting if she wished.

But Marigold's comment about the sight for sore eyes didn't make sense. "The refill on the water pitcher, you mean? Yeah, we all need to stay hydrated. This heat is ridiculous." Clementine poured filtered tap water into the serving pitcher.

"No, dear, I meant your smile. I haven't seen it since the festival."

"We can't have that, can we?" It had been a rough week and a half since she last saw Liam, but that didn't mean Clementine had nothing to smile about. The world was a beautiful place. She need only look out her kitchen window for confirmation of God's activity in the world.

Beneath the shady trees, ewes and lambs rested on the cool grass, Dolley and Martha keeping them company, while Rex and Fergus tightened the hinges on the south paddock gate. "Who would have thought, even ten days ago, that Fergus would be lending a hand at Honeysuckle Farm?"

"God, of course. Just like He knew there's gold on the farm." Marigold joined her at the sink to look out the window. "Have you spoken to anyone about it?"

"Joel Morgan. He doesn't do this type of law, but he referred me to a person familiar with mineral rights. I've also shown an expert what Fergus panned from the creek, and I'm splitting it with him. Calling it a finder's fee. Anyway, despite what Fergus said about a vein, I'm not expecting much." Clementine wiped condensation off the pitcher with a clean towel.

"It's exciting to think about, though, isn't it?" Marigold's smile turned shy when she caught sight of Rex through the window. "God has lots of surprises in store, doesn't He? Look at me. I thought I was done with romance. Then I got to talking with Rex, and well, I kept our friendship a secret in case it turned out to be folly. Can't deny it any longer, though. I'm no spring chicken, but that man out there makes me weak in the knees."

"I am sure it's mutual." Clementine couldn't help but grin. "You two are adorable."

"You and Liam were adorable, too." Marigold sighed. "This may come as a surprise to you, but when I pushed Liam into helping you with the festival, I had an ulterior motive."

Clementine burst into laughter. "You're a notorious matchmaker, Marigold. I sort of figured."

Marigold looked almost offended. "Sometimes when people are bullheaded, subtle doesn't work. But in this case, I should've kept my nose out of it. Too much water under the bridge, and there were kids involved. I hate that I got their hopes up. Were they devastated when he left?"

"They're okay. Honest." It had broken Clementine's already fractured heart that the kids had hoped Liam might be their uncle, and for a few days, Wynn had been extra quiet and Annie, extra cranky. They'd started to bounce back, though, and last week, they'd received some good news that distracted them. "My parents are coming for an extended visit this summer. It's given us all something to look forward to."

"Wonderful." Marigold's smile turned sad again. "But again, I'm sorry I meddled."

Clementine offered a one-armed hug—the best she could do with the pitcher in hand. "God brought good things out of Liam's return to Widow's Peak Creek. Thanks to his encouragement, I'm going to start blogging about the sheep. It's small, but a first step toward writing more agricultural articles once Annie is a little older."

"I'm so glad. All I ever wanted was for you to be happy. And Liam to be happy."

"We are. I'm happy with my sheep, and he's happy scaling cliffs. Those two things don't go together, but that's okay."

"Sometimes, odd combinations work, though. Like cucumber slices in water." Marigold tapped the pitcher. "I always thought cucumbers were for salads and pickles."

"I've been told it's a spa-type thing."

"Fancy. But refreshing."

At the sounds of the front door opening and closing, Clementine tipped her head toward the family room. "Sounds like Faith is here."

Marigold accompanied her, reaching out to kiss Faith on the cheek. "How are you feeling, Mama-to-be?"

"Better." Faith smiled, hand on her still-flat tummy.

Setting down the pitcher, Clementine welcomed Faith and joined in the chitchat about the Santos baby coming in November. The last thing she wanted was for Faith to get overheated, though, so at the next lull in the conversation, she spread out her hands. "Looks like we're all here. Shall we get started, Gretchen?"

"Absolutely." Gretchen stopped fanning herself with

a festival map. "I'll start with a recap and financial report, and then each of us will share on our particular areas. Clementine, no need to cover Liam's activities. I've included that in my report."

"I'm happy to do it myself." A masculine voice carried from the threshold.

Liam?

He was supposed to be on a plane to Indonesia right now, but he was here, in her house. In his dark gray T-shirt, jeans and boots, he looked hot—warm, that is, not... Well, he did look handsome as ever, his hair mussed, his eyes sparking. And oh, his smile did things to make her ankles wobble.

"You're not on a plane" was all she managed to say.

"I couldn't do it."

What did he mean, he couldn't? Had he forgotten his passport? Was his collarbone giving him more trouble since the incident with Fergus?

Kellan rose to shake his hand. "If you wanted to submit a report for the committee, there's such a thing as email, you know."

"Some things, a man has to take care of himself." Liam's gaze glued on to Clementine's, but he broke contact when his grandma stood on tiptoe to kiss him. "Hi, Grandma. Sorry to come back without warning you, but I didn't think you'd mind the surprise."

"I was just telling Clementine how wonderful surprises can be." She tugged her ear. "I didn't hear you come in the front door."

Faith smiled. "He snuck in with me and I promised to let him make a grand entrance."

"How's Annie's arm?" The way Liam looked at

Clementine, it was like they were the only two people in the room.

"Fine. Good. Used to the cast now."

"Back to the meeting." Gretchen indicated Liam should sit on the couch beside her chair, but Marigold plopped into the spare seat, leaving the loveseat free for Clementine and Liam. After a sharp, annoyed-sounding intake of breath, Gretchen called things to order and recapped the festival events before drawing their attention to the financial report.

Wow. They'd made a great profit, but Clementine could hardly concentrate on the good numbers with Liam beside her. Why had he come back, and why did he look so happy? He was supposed to be thirty thousand feet in the air and—oh, it was time for their report.

Clementine reiterated the numbers she'd furnished to Gretchen on income they'd made off the vendor fair. "If the festival comes back next year, I recommend expanding the vendor sale from one day to three. Some people came on Saturday expressly for the shopping but, naturally, enjoyed the other festival offerings while they were there."

"Agreed," Liam added. "It will increase the revenue for the festival, too, since the vendors gave a percentage of profits to the cause, instead of a fee."

"And the recipe contest?" Gretchen's brow quirked. "I heard it wasn't interesting."

Kellan pulled a face. "I'm not sure where you heard that, but it was a blast. And I'm not just saying that because Marigold's fantastic cake won."

"Well, Mayor Hughes said it wasn't anything special. If it's not something a lot of people care about, we shouldn't do it next year." Gretchen made a large slash on her paper with a pen, as if cancelling the recipe contest.

Clementine didn't care for the smug look on their leader's face. "On the contrary, there was such an interest in the recipes that I recommend creating a Gold Rush Days cookbook. With proceeds going to the town heritage fund, of course. There could be sections devoted to prizewinning recipes, town favorites and maybe even a vintage-recipe section, just for fun."

"I can help with vintage recipes." Faith set down her water glass. "I'd be delighted to sell the cookbook in the antiques store, too."

Kellan poured himself more water. "It's a great idea. I'd carry it at Open Book, and I guarantee we'd sell them to townspeople and tourists alike."

Liam leaned forward. "Would you be willing to include your top-secret marmalade cake recipe, Grandma?"

"For a charitable cause? Indeed I would, and I'm sure Rex will share the ingredients of his corn concoction, too."

Lips spread in a thin smile, Gretchen took notes. Clementine didn't mind if Gretchen hated the idea, or even if she never liked Clementine much. Clementine would still extend a hand of friendship.

When the business had finished, Gretchen tapped her pen against her clipboard. "One final question. Would you all be interested in serving again next year?"

A resounding yes chorused through the room from everyone but Liam and Faith. Her hand turned palm up. "The baby's due in November. I want to help, but I'm not sure how hands-on I can be with a six-month-old baby."

Kellan chuckled. "As the parent of an almost-seven-month-old? Let's talk later."

The others laughed, but Clementine could hardly focus enough to engage. She kept sneaking peeks at Liam. Curiosity at his presence burned a hole in her stomach.

"All right, then." Gretchen clicked her pen. "We're adjourned."

"Wait." Liam held up a hand. "I'm happy to help out next year."

Clementine's throat went drier than the Mojave Desert. "You are?"

"Happier than I've been in a long, long time. So happy I had to turn around at the airport and drive straight here to tell you."

That burning hole of curiosity in Clementine's stomach? It set her entire being alight with a blazing fire of shock and wonder.

Kellan stood up. "Look at the time. I need to get back to Main Street."

"Me, too." Faith gathered her purse. "Great meeting, everyone." Then she met Clementine's gaze and mouthed "call me later."

Sure, if she were capable of functioning later. Right now, Clementine was a weak-kneed, confused bundle of nerves, but one thing was clear.

She wasn't finished with Liam Murphy. Not by a long shot.

Public displays of emotion or affection had never been Liam's style, but he didn't care if the whole world knew how he felt. Or what he was about to do.

First things first, though. "How much time before you have to pick up Annie from school?"

"She's going home with a friend today. I'll get her after Wynn comes home."

Clementine's nervous lick of her lips told him she was uncertain about what was happening right now, but he wasn't. He would say what he came to say, and then if she wanted, he'd get back in his car. Forever, this time.

"Want to take a walk?" He tipped his head in the direction of the fields.

They ended up strolling toward Blue Creek. The sheep gathered beneath trees for shade from the blistering sun, Dolley in their midst. Martha was there, too, and while she didn't leave her shady spot to greet him, her tail thumped on the grass.

"Where did Fergus and Rex go?" Clementine scanned the area. "They were just here."

"Maybe they left with Grandma. I heard her say something about an early lunch. I'm so glad Fergus has changed his ways. He has, hasn't he?"

"Oh, yes. He's helping around here, and he and Rex have clicked. I'm so glad Fergus is making friends. I think he's been alone a long time."

She led him beneath the trees lining the creek. Over the bubbling water, she filled him in on her plans to look for gold in the area Fergus had found. "We'll dig a little bit, but I don't want to spoil this." She gestured at the natural wonder around her.

"I've traveled all over the world, but this has to be one of the prettiest places I've ever seen. But." He paused, taking a breath.

"But? You think I should dig it all up for gold?"

"No, sweetheart." He pivoted so he faced her, looking

down into the blue eyes that had captivated his heart so many years ago. "I meant that the loveliness of this place pales in comparison to you. Never in my whole life has anything ever taken my breath away. Except for you."

He could hardly breathe now, looking at her.

It didn't seem like he was alone in his struggle to inhale, because Clementine's breath hitched. "I don't understand."

He cupped her cheek, thumb tracing the supple skin beneath her lips. "I've spent years running from my feelings, always afraid to return to Widow's Peak Creek because I knew I'd have to face them here. Memories of my parents. My disappointments and failures. Sure enough, being here hurt, but it also made me see some new things about myself. Like how happy I am with you and the kids. How miserable I am without you. I love you, Clementine, and I'm going to love you with the last breath I take on this earth. I want to be with you."

"But your job—"

"I gave it up." Nothing had ever been so easy to do.

"No." She pulled away from his touch, leaving him hollow and cold. "You can't. I won't let you."

Clementine's thoughts tangled into a jumbled mess. Liam loved her?

Her heart had leaped at the words and then cracked right down the middle again. "Your job is your life. That's not an understatement. It's your everything."

"I've parted ways with Javier and his global projects, Clementine, and I don't regret it."

"But you will." Didn't he understand that? "Maybe not for a year, but in five? Ten? You'll grow dissatisfied, maybe even bitter. God made you with an adventurous spirit. I could never ask you to be someone other than who you are."

"You didn't ask. This is my choice."

"But it won't work." She could no longer deny the truth to herself, or him. "I still love you. I never stopped. I thought I had. I thought I was over you, but I know now I will never be over you. But if I love you, that means I have to let you go."

"You love me?" He reached for her hand. Pressed it to his lips.

It was hard to think with the pressure of his lips sending currents of electricity up her arm. "Even though I knew we were on different paths, even though I fought it, my feelings only deepened. But love isn't enough."

"I don't think we're on different paths, sweetheart."

"How can you say that? Look at us. Look at me. I'm working on my anxiety, but I don't know how long I'll struggle with it. I wish I could say I'm fine with you scaling volcanoes to get footage, but I'm not. I may have climbed that ladder to get Wynn, but I still have a long way to go. You can't put your life on hold until I'm okay with you taking risks, because I might never get there."

"I'm not putting my life on hold, but considering California has twenty volcanoes, I'll be in their vicinities at one point or another in my new job. No more unnecessary risks to get shots, though, I promise. I have too much to lose. In fact—"

"New job?"

Liam's smile twitched up on the left side. "Maybe I should have told you that part first. I was at the airport for my red-eye, bags in hand, but I didn't have a shred of peace. I decided it was time to step out in faith. I went back home to pick up a few things, got in my car and started driving here to you. Once it was business hours, I called my representative, and in something only God could do, it turns out a group dedicated to capturing America's natural wonders on film liked my work and had just inquired if I was available for a long-term assignment based in Northern California. There's still some travel involved but never too far from Widow's Peak Creek, so I can live here. If you're concerned about my safety, you need to know that taking risks doesn't sound the least bit interesting to me. You and the kids are more than enough adventure for me. But if you want me to, I'll turn down the job and do something else, because I know that what I do—what I've done—scares you."

It did. But the steps he'd taken to be with her overwhelmed her with love and care. It couldn't have been an easy choice for him to walk away from his job security, but he'd done so, willingly. And God had provided for him. Couldn't she take a step of faith, too?

"Remember when Lady Bird and her babies got stuck in the berry brambles?"

It was such an abrupt change of topic, it was little wonder Liam looked confused. "Fergus had cut the fence to cause trouble."

"That's right, but I was just thinking of how easy it was to get Lady Bird out of the bushes because she didn't fight me. Bo Peep put up such a fuss, though. She fought because she was scared." Clementine could feel her heart pounding in her chest. "I've been fighting, too. Fighting God because of my fear. I can't promise I won't worry, but it's time to trust God with the things that scare me. This seems like a way for you to do what you love but also have a home base in Widow's Peak Creek. And if it's what you want, oh, I want it, too."

"You are my home, Clem, no matter what I do for a living." His finger tipped her chin up, lifting her gaze to his. "Will you have me? I know it won't always be easy. I don't know how to raise kids."

"I didn't, either, but Wynn and Annie just want to be loved."

"I love them already, but that doesn't mean I won't make mistakes. I don't know how to be a husband, either, but I promise to fight for you, for us." His hand slid down her arm, leaving a trail of fire in its wake. "I meant it when I asked if you'd have me. I didn't just mean for now. I meant forever, Clementine. I want a family with you, Wynn and Annie. And Grandma and Rex. And Martha and Dolley and all the sheep, now and in the future, until we run out of First Lady names for them. There would be no greater honor in my life than being your husband."

Oh my word.

He lifted her hand to his lips yet again. "Clementine Simon, will you marry me?"

He smiled, but there was still a sliver of fear in his eyes. This man was as scared as she was but had taken steps of faith to be what she needed. He held her heart yesterday, today and always. Life was a risk, yes, but some risks were worth taking.

"Yes, Liam. Oh, yes."

In one glorious moment he pulled her to him, their smiling gazes locked. And then her eyes shut as her lips met his. She'd forgotten how wonderful it was to be kissed by Liam, held close, feeling his heart pounding beneath her palm.

Yet this kiss—no, kisses, were different than they used to be, too. These were filled with joy and promise.

Epilogue

Honeysuckle Farm had never looked better.

The view of the Sierra Nevada was majestic, the summer evening was mild, and her friends had outdone themselves decorating her patio and yard. Pale green ribbons tied to the fence posts fluttered in the breeze, and the dining area set up beneath the white canopy beside the patio was like a page out of a magazine. With a rug underfoot and a chandelier hanging above, the tables were gorgeous, decked out with flameless candles and vases of white roses and baby's breath.

A year ago—even six months ago—Clementine would never have imagined she'd have such a lovely rehearsal dinner the night before her wedding.

Nor could she have imagined the groom would be the one she'd loved for so long but thought she could never have.

Liam looked handsome in his pale blue button-down shirt and chinos as he talked to her dad, Rex and Fergus by the beverage station. Then his gaze met hers, sending her stomach into flutters.

Marigold blocked her view of her dashing fiancé as

she set down her marmalade cake at one end of the buffet table. Clementine hurried to move a plate of cookies a few inches to give the cake more room. "Is that the last of the food?" The roast chicken, rice pilaf, mashed root vegetables and salads were catered, but Clementine's friends insisted on providing desserts.

"It sure is." Clementine's mother stuck tongs into one of the salads. With her dark blond hair and gray eyes, she resembled Annie and Brielle.

"Everything looks amazing." Wrapping her arm around her mother's waist, she squeezed. "I can't get over these decorations."

"There's a lot to celebrate." Marigold adjusted the knife beside her marmalade cake. "This might have been a short engagement, but this marriage was years in the making. And involved a whole lot of praying by certain people, I might add."

The ladies gathered around all chuckled, but a short engagement worked best for everyone's schedules. Clementine's parents were already visiting from Africa, the kids were on summer vacation, and Liam and Clementine were ready to start their lives together.

"I like how God answered your prayers, Marigold." Clementine gave her friend—soon to be her grandmother-in-law—a kiss on the cheek. Then she turned her smile on to Liam's mom, Barbara. "I'm so glad you're here, too."

Barbara's relationships with her kids were improving slowly but surely. After leaving Widow's Peak Creek the way she did sixteen years ago, Barbara admitted to Liam she was wary of how others might treat her, but Marigold and Clementine had made overtures toward forging new relationships with her. It would take time, but Clementine had faith Barbara and her children would find their way back to being a closer family again.

Barbara's hand went to her heart. "I couldn't miss Liam getting married. And then to find out Sara's expecting? Turned out to be a bigger weekend than I thought."

Sara and Dane had started attending church, and their marriage was stronger than ever. They'd decided together they wanted to be parents, and they looked toward their little one's arrival with joy.

Faith Santos squeezed Leah Dean's shoulder. "In a few weeks, we'll have another celebration when you're the bride."

"I can't wait." Leah's eyes were full of love when she looked at her fiancé. "I thank God for Benton every day."

Benton had done a lot to help Clementine the past few weeks, listening as she shared her anxieties, praying and referring her to a professional who could better guide her. No one had championed her fight against anxiety, though, like Liam. His tender care gave her strength and confidence, and she'd managed to get through his work trip in the High Sierra without a single panic attack.

It wasn't that she hadn't worried at all, but she trusted him to not take unnecessary risks while filming. And she trusted God to shepherd her family, no matter what life brought their way.

The past few months had been full of surprises. Liam loved his new job and coworkers. Her improved website had helped her business grow, and her blogs on the sheep had caught the attention of a local agricultural group who wanted to feature her articles. Fergus had been a huge support with the installation of her new fence and had started coming to church. As for the gold he'd suspected lay under her pond? They'd found enough to start funds for the kids' futures. Clementine was grateful for God's provision.

"Hey."

She turned to find Liam reaching for her hand. She took it in both of hers. "Hey, yourself. I was just thinking about you."

"No surprise there," Paige teased.

"What were you thinking?" Marigold looked completely serious. "That he should shave that beard off by tomorrow? Because he has the sweetest dimples hiding under all that scruff."

Laughing, Clementine pulled Liam closer by the hand. "I was thinking that everyone we love is here. And tomorrow we'll be married. All I ever wanted, Liam."

"Me, too, Clementine." He kissed her fingers.

"If you lovebirds don't mind, the food's getting cold," Rex joked, pretending to be perturbed. "Benton's ready to pray and you two are getting gushy."

"Yeah, gushy." Wynn pulled a face as he marched to Liam's side.

"We should pray and not be gushy anymore." Annie rushed to Clementine, reaching for her hand, and Wynn did the same with Liam.

Before they bowed their heads, Liam squeezed her hand three times. *I-love-you.* A glance showed her he did the same to Wynn's hand. She squeezed back and did the same three-squeeze pattern to Annie.

They were about to officially become a family. Tomorrow, she and Liam would promise to love and honor one another all the days of their lives.

And she couldn't wait to get started.

* * * * *

If you enjoyed this story,
look for these other books
by Susanne Dietze:

A Future for His Twins
Seeking Sanctuary
A Small-Town Christmas Challenge

Dear Reader,

Sometimes readers ask where story ideas come from. Would you believe this story was inspired by a bar of soap? While I'd heard of goat's milk soap, I didn't know about sheep's milk soap until recently. I love trying new soaps, so I had to try it.

Perhaps at some point you've been in an anxious period, like Clementine. I certainly have. In difficult times, I pray we're all reminded anew how tender, compassionate, and trustworthy our Shepherd is. He gently invites us to cast our cares on Him. To rest in Him. To accept the peace only He can give.

I'm so excited to be back soon with another book set in Widow's Peak Creek. I think Joel Morgan deserves a happily-ever-after, don't you?

Until then, I'd love to connect. You can reach me through my website, www.SusanneDietze.com, and find all my social media handles there. You can also subscribe to my electronic newsletter.

Thank you for picking up this book! You've blessed my socks off!

Blessings to you and yours,
Susanne

LOVE INSPIRED

Stories to uplift and inspire

Fall in love with Love Inspired—
inspirational and uplifting stories of faith
and hope. Find strength and comfort in
the bonds of friendship and community.
Revel in the warmth of possibility and the
promise of new beginnings.

Sign up for the Love Inspired newsletter
at **LoveInspired.com** to be the first
to find out about upcoming titles,
special promotions and exclusive content.

CONNECT WITH US AT:

 Facebook.com/LoveInspiredBooks

Twitter.com/LoveInspiredBks

THE AMISH MATCHMAKER'S CHOICE
Redemption's Amish Legacies • by Patricia Johns
Newly returned to the Amish community, Jake Knussli must find a wife in
six months or lose his uncle's farm. Can matchmaker Adel Draschel secure
a *frau* for him—before losing her own heart to the handsome farmer?

THEIR PRETEND COURTSHIP
The Amish of New Hope • by Carrie Lighte
Pressured by her stepfather to court, Eliza Keim begrudgingly walks out
with blueberry farmer Jonas Kanagy—except Jonas is only trying to protect
his brother from what he thinks are Eliza's heartbreaker ways. When the
two are forced to make their courtship in name only look real, they may
discover more than they bargained for...

GUARDING HIS SECRET
K-9 Companions • by Jill Kemerer
When Wyoming rancher Randy Watkins finds himself caring for his surprise
baby nephew, he seeks the help of longtime friend Hannah Carr. But when
her retired service dog seems to sense all is not right with Randy's health,
will he trust Hannah with the truth?

THE RANCHER'S FAMILY LEGACY
The Ranchers of Gabriel Bend • by Myra Johnson
Building contractor Mark Caldwell is ready to inherit his grandfather's
horse ranch and put his traumatic past behind him—if he can survive
working in Texas Hill Country for a year. But when his dog bonds with local
caterer Holly Elliot's son, can they put aside their differences and open
their hearts?

HER MOUNTAIN REFUGE
by Laurel Blount
Widowed, pregnant and under the thumb of her controlling mother-in-law,
Charlotte Tremaine needs help—but she doesn't expect it to come from
her estranged childhood best friend. Yet letting Sheriff Logan Carter whisk
her away to his foster mother's remote mountain home might be her best
chance at a fresh start...

A MOTHER FOR HIS SON
by Betty Woods
In town to help her grandmother, chef Rachel Landry plans to use the time
to heal her broken heart—not help Mac Greer with his guest ranch. But
her growing affection for his little boy could be just the push she needs to
once again see the possibility of something more...

LICNM0422

Get 4 FREE REWARDS!

We'll send you 2 FREE Books plus 2 FREE Mystery Gifts.

Both the **Love Inspired®** and **Love Inspired®** Suspense series feature compelling novels filled with inspirational romance, faith, forgiveness, and hope.

YES! Please send me 2 FREE novels from the Love Inspired or Love Inspired Suspense series and my 2 FREE gifts (gifts are worth about $10 retail). After receiving them, if I don't wish to receive any more books, I can return the shipping statement marked "cancel." If I don't cancel, I will receive 6 brand-new Love Inspired Larger-Print books or Love Inspired Suspense Larger-Print books every month and be billed just $5.99 each in the U.S. or $6.24 each in Canada. That is a savings of at least 17% off the cover price. It's quite a bargain! Shipping and handling is just 50¢ per book in the U.S. and $1.25 per book in Canada.* I understand that accepting the 2 free books and gifts places me under no obligation to buy anything. I can always return a shipment and cancel at any time. The free books and gifts are mine to keep no matter what I decide.

Choose one: ☐ **Love Inspired**   ☐ **Love Inspired Suspense**
                    Larger-Print   **Larger-Print**
                    (122/322 IDN GNWC)   (107/307 IDN GNWN)

Name (please print)

Address   Apt. #

City   State/Province   Zip/Postal Code

Email: Please check this box ☐ if you would like to receive newsletters and promotional emails from Harlequin Enterprises ULC and its affiliates. You can unsubscribe anytime.

Mail to the Harlequin Reader Service:
IN U.S.A.: P.O. Box 1341, Buffalo, NY 14240-8531
IN CANADA: P.O. Box 603, Fort Erie, Ontario L2A 5X3

Want to try 2 free books from another series? Call 1-800-873-8635 or visit www.ReaderService.com.

*Terms and prices subject to change without notice. Prices do not include sales taxes, which will be charged (if applicable) based on your state or country of residence. Canadian residents will be charged applicable taxes. Offer not valid in Quebec. This offer is limited to one order per household. Books received may not be as shown. Not valid for current subscribers to the Love Inspired or Love Inspired Suspense series. All orders subject to approval. Credit or debit balances in a customer's account(s) may be offset by any other outstanding balance owed by or to the customer. Please allow 4 to 6 weeks for delivery. Offer available while quantities last.

Your Privacy—Your information is being collected by Harlequin Enterprises ULC, operating as Harlequin Reader Service. For a complete summary of the information we collect, how we use this information and to whom it is disclosed, please visit our privacy notice located at corporate.harlequin.com/privacy-notice. From time to time we may also exchange your personal information with reputable third parties. If you wish to opt out of this sharing of your personal information, please visit readerservice.com/consumerschoice or call 1-800-873-8635. **Notice to California Residents**—Under California law, you have specific rights to control and access your data. For more information on these rights and how to exercise them, visit corporate.harlequin.com/california-privacy.

LIRLIS22

"What do I need to know?" Hannah faced him then, her big blue eyes full of expectation. Randy liked that about her. She didn't hide anything.

Well, everyone hid something. He'd certainly been hiding something for years—from this town, from his friends, even from his brother.

So what? It was nobody's business.

"Let's start with the basics." He gave her a quick tour. Her presence was making his pulse race. He didn't like it or the reason why it was happening.

Hannah's cell phone rang. "Do you mind if I take this?"

"Go ahead." He backed up to give her privacy, busying himself with a box of nets, but he could hear every word she said.

"You're kidding," she said breathlessly. "That's great news. Yes…Right now? I'd love to…You're serious? I can't believe it…"

Finally, she ended the conversation and turned to him with shining eyes. "That was Molly. She has a dog for me."

"Another puppy?" He placed the box on the counter.

"No, a retired service dog." She looked ready to float through the air. "I've been on the adoption list forever. The ones that have become available all went to either their original puppy raiser or someone higher on the list."

"Won't the dog be old?" Why would she want someone's ancient dog that might not live long?

"Some of them are. This one is eight. Too old to be placed for service, but he's still got a lot of good years left."

Something told him that even if the dog had only a couple of good months left, Hannah would be equally enthusiastic.

"I'm going to go pick him up." She lightly clapped her hands in happiness, and he kind of wished he could go with her.

"Let me get you the store key, then."

"Oh, wait." She winced. "I didn't think this through. Is there any way I can bring him with me to the store? He passed all of his obedience classes years ago. I'm sure he wouldn't cause any trouble. I just can't imagine bringing him home and then leaving him by himself all day before he has a chance to get to know me. He's used to being with someone all the time."

"Of course. Bring him." He'd always liked dogs. His customers wouldn't mind. In fact, they'd probably linger in the store even more because of him. Maybe he'd get a dog of his own after he moved into the new house. It was a thought.

"Thanks." She came over and gave him a quick hug. "I'll open the store tomorrow at nine. You're closed on Sundays, right?"

"Right." He stood frozen from the shock of her touch as she hurried to the back. The sound of the screen door slamming jolted him out of his stupor.

Hannah almost made him forget he wasn't like any other guy.

And he wasn't.

He had a secret. And that secret would stay with him until the day he died.

When that day came, he'd be single.

He had to be more careful around Hannah Carr. There was something about her that made his logic disappear like the morning dew. He couldn't afford to forget he couldn't have her.

Don't miss Guarding His Secret
by Jill Kemerer, available June 2022
wherever Love Inspired books and ebooks are sold.

LoveInspired.com

LIEXP0422